IMMORTAL PERIL

An Immortal Story of True Love, Disaster, and Peril

The Immortal Stories Series

Book 3

by

Linda Ashton Trott

Tagger Press

Copyright

ISBN-13: 978-1-7781131-8-5

Cover design by: 100COVERS

First Edition, July 2022

Adult Content, 18+

Dedication

I am dedicating this book to my husband, who without, it would have been impossible to complete this work.

A huge thank you to Lee Burton for being my editor. On my second book, I am still learning and he is a very good teacher and editor.

Thanks to you the reader as well, for purchasing this book. I hope you enjoy it! If you do, don't forget to leave a review.

A special mention to my #1 fan for a fantastic suggestion to the plot — way to go Sam!

Contents

Copyright . . . . -ii-

Dedication . . . . -iii-

Contents . . . . -iv-

What you Missed . . . . -vi-

Chapter 1 . . . . -1-

Chapter 2 . . . . -4-

Chapter 3 . . . . -13-

Chapter 4 . . . . -30-

Chapter 5 . . . . -33-

Chapter 6 . . . . -54-

Chapter 7 . . . . -67-

Chapter 8 . . . . -71-

Chapter 9 . . . . -75-

Chapter 10 . . . . -89-

Chapter 11 . . . . -99-

Chapter 12 . . . . -103-

Chapter 13 . . . . -120-

Chapter 14 . . . . -127-

Chapter 15 . . . . -141-

Chapter 16 . . . . -146-

Chapter 17 . . . . -154-

Chapter 18 . . . . -163-

Chapter 19 . . . . -177-

Chapter 20 . . . . -183-

Chapter 21 . . . . -186-

Chapter 22 . . . . -192-

Chapter 23 . . . . -196-

Chapter 24 . . . . -209-

Chapter 25 . . . . -219-

Excerpt from Book 4 . . . . -228-

What's Next? . . . . -238-

About The Author . . . . -239-

Books In This Series . . . . -240-

Praise for the Series . . . . -243-

Being an Indie Author . . . . -246-

What you Missed

In the previous Immortal Story

- Falon had to recover from learning Mark was Zisis
- Falon decided to experience more lovers and have fun
- Falon had some fun with the hotel band
- Falon got to see her favorite band play live, twice
- A road trip with a sexy pastry chef
- A nasty encounter that Mark rescued her from
- A romantic night on a roof with a hot tub
- Playing footsie during a conference
- Foursome road trip to Miami to party
- A big makeup scene, big

Chapter 1

— Rick

Justin wanted to do something special for our restaurant's New Year's Eve celebration. After winning the James Beard award last August, the restaurant had become busier than ever, so we hired a full-time manager to handle the day-to-day operations and increase our chef staff. Justin still set the menus and designed the cuisine, but there were now two executive chefs who did all the work.

I was feeling something was missing for the celebrations, and it was Lora. After that amazing visit in October for the Hallowe'en party, I was missing her terribly. I realized I was rather addicted to her already. Her scent, the feel of her skin, how she loved me … I didn't want to be without her anymore.

Phone calls didn't cut it either. I'd tried to bury myself in the business, which helped a lot. However, when I was alone, it was empty. I missed her smile, her lovely eyes, and especially her wicked sense of humor. I loved the way she flirted with not-so-subtle innuendo and was not afraid to back it up with action.

So many women flirted, suggested, but when it came down to it, they were not prepared to do what they proposed. Lora always followed through, so far at least. She was as adventurous as I was—she hadn't said no to anything yet.

Maybe I should give her a call and see if I could get her down to Atlanta again. I knew she was on a tight budget, and raising three kids was difficult on a single parent's salary. I had no problem paying for her travel; after all, I was comfortably well off. I could always bring them all down and then have Mama Anita babysit them at night when I took Lora out. But maybe she would rather stay with her kids.

I'd offer her either option. It didn't matter to me, as long as I got to see her. Pulling her business card out, I gave her a call.

"Lora O'Reilly speaking, how may I help you today?" came her lovely voice.

"The accent isn't as noticeable today," I replied. "I kind of miss it."

"Rick! Oh, what a pleasure hearing from you!" she exclaimed. "I was just thinking about you and our last phone call."

"That's nice to hear!" I said, as a memory of that call flashed in my mind, bringing back the heat I'd felt during our telephone sex. "I was hoping to convince you to come down again to Atlanta. It has been a while since we saw each other."

"I didn't know we were 'seeing each other,'" Lora said. A little nervous butterfly started flapping in my gut. *Why?* "That's still a little way off for me. It's what, six weeks away?"

"Why don't we start seeing each other?" I countered.

"Rick, I live twelve hundred miles away. How do we see each other?" Lora asked. "I'm not into long distance relationships. They never work out."

"Lora, I'm not going to beat around the bush. I'm a wealthy man," I said. "I want to be with you as often as possible, and I'm willing to pay for your travel expenses or fly to see you. I just can't let you go. You've touched my soul. You've captured my heart. Not to mention the sex with you is, well, I don't want to be with another woman, ever. I want to see where this can go. Where we can go."

"Oh," said Lora.

The line went silent for a minute.

"Lora? Are you still there?"

"Sorry, I was thinking about what you said," she said. "Okay, here's what I think: I want to see where this goes too. I'm just concerned about my kids, and how this is all going to work. I don't want to bring another man into their lives if it's not going somewhere. Does that make sense? And their father is an asshole, so I have to deal with that too."

"Yes, it does. So, can we see if it goes somewhere?" I asked. "I felt so much for you so quickly, I need to know if my mind is leading me on or if it is real."

"Agreed. Let's see if this chemistry between us is really a thing," she suggested.

I let out the breath I didn't know I was holding.

"Okay, Justin and I are having a big party event for New Year's," I said. "Would you like to come down for the New Year's Eve party? You can bring the kids, have a vacation with them here. I can book flights for you. You can come down after work, on Friday night or even Saturday morning once the kids are off school."

"As always, I have to find out what the kids' father is doing. I will get back to you as soon as I can. Okay?"

"Good," I answered. "I look forward to it."

"Bye!"

Chapter 2

— Lora

Getting off the phone, I was tingling all over. That man really turned me on something fierce!

I needed to do a calming ritual to get my spirit back under control before trying to speak to Bruce. He was so exasperating that I needed to be very centered and calm. I would wait until I got home tonight to do this.

At home, the usual things pulled my attention: getting the kids doing their homework, picking up after them and getting dinner on. It wasn't until after dinner and the dishes were loaded into the dishwasher, that I felt I had the head space to take on this challenge.

I walked into my meditation room, lit my candles, and put some white sage in my incense burner. Burning white sage helped cleanse my spirit and calm the butterflies trying to get out of my heart. Twenty minutes later, I was calm and centered. Now I could speak to the kids' father.

I checked the calendar; there were no plans marked on it yet for the end of the year. And it appeared it was his weekend anyway. *Well, that's good news.* Perhaps the idiot would take the kids after all. Wouldn't that be nice. It depended on whether or not his girlfriend was working. She was a stripper, and she took side jobs.

I was an exotic dancer in my younger years. It was a great way to make money, lots of it. I put myself through university stripping. But I had a cardinal rule: I never did side jobs and I never took "dates" with customers. As an exotic dancer, I took pride in my ability to tantalize and titillate, but I was a no-touch dancer. And once I got pregnant with my first child, I stopped altogether. I never wanted the kids exposed to that world.

Shiree, on the other hand, was a touch-me dancer. I knew she had johns and private customers. I hated that they exposed my kids to that crap, but I couldn't do anything about it.

I called Bruce, my kids' father, and got his voicemail. So I left a message about New Year's, telling him that I was invited out of town, and was wondering if he was still taking the kids since it was his time with them.

Bruce called me back a couple of hours later.

"Lora, why do I have to cover your ass again with the kids?" demanded Bruce as a way of greeting me on the phone.

"You're not, idiot," I replied. "You are supposed to take the kids for a week starting the Saturday after Christmas. That goes until the Friday after New Year's. I'm simply confirming that you are indeed taking the kids, because I have plans."

"You have plans," he commented. "Well, hoity toity, you have plans. What about me and my plans?"

"Look, are you taking the kids that week or not?"

"Yes, but I promised Shiree a vacation. So we're taking the kids skiing."

"That will be nice for them. You do remember that they don't own ski gear, right?"

"Yeah, I remember. They'll rent the equipment at the hill. We're booked in at Mont Tremblant."

"Excellent," I said. "Do you mind taking them a day earlier? I have a flight out on Saturday."

"Yeah, I can be there by 8:00 on Friday to pick them up. When is your flight?"

"I don't know exactly, but it will be in the afternoon," I said. "Thank you."

I called Rick back right away. "Hey you!" I said when Rick answered the phone. "I can come down! Bruce will pick up the kids on Friday night. He's taking them all skiing."

"Wonderful! I'll book the flight for you immediately," said Rick. "What day would you like to fly?"

"Let's make it on Saturday afternoon."

"Perfect! We can have nearly a whole week together."

"Thank you for the invitation," I said. "Sure beats being cold up here in Montreal! And it's a great reason to go shopping for some new sexy lingerie."

Rick grunted. "I can just imagine you in sexy lingerie. Now what am I going to do?"

Giggling, I said sweetly, "Oh my, are you having a problem?"

"No, no problem," he said, sounding like he was gritting his teeth. "Nothing you couldn't solve for me anyway."

"Rick,"

"Yes, Lora?"

"I'm alone in my office and I don't have any appointments for the next thirty minutes," I said suggestively. "Should I close the door and make sure I'm not interrupted?"

"I'm not alone, but I can be. Give me a minute," he said, moving from the hallway into his office and closing the door. "Okay, I'm alone in my office now."

I made sure the office door was locked. There were no windows except outside, so no one saw me on the thirteenth floor. I laid down on the couch.

"Rick…"

"Lora…" His voice got thick.

"I'm undoing my blouse," I said seductively. "Slowly."

"What kind of closure does it have?"

"It's a zipper," I said. "As I'm pulling it down slowly, I'm dragging my fingertip down my skin. It's giving me shivers as I pass between my breasts. My nipples are getting happy."

A soft moan escaped his lips.

"Mmm," he said. "I can imagine running my finger down your body and sending those shivers. I can see your nipples becoming stimulated. That makes me feel like touching my own nipples too."

My breath stuttered as my nipples responded and the coil inside me tightened.

"I'm getting so wet," I murmured. "I've reached the bottom of the zipper. I'm now pulling the sides apart to expose my bra. It's a cream colored, very sheer, demi-cup, that barely contains my nipples."

He sucked in his breath and moaned again. "You wore that to work?" he asked with a thick voice. "I can imagine watching you walk around with that on and being able to see your nipples all day. Oh now I'm so excited my cock has grown two inches."

I groaned again; I heard the rustling of his fabric as he stimulated himself. I unzipped my pants too.

I could hear his groans on the other end of the phone. It added a sense of urgency and reality.

"I've licked my finger and I'm flicking my nipple, making it wet," I said, as my nipple popped up and became very hard. "My nipples have become so sensitive, Rick. I am pinching them and wish you were sucking on them."

"Oh, Lora, I am visualizing my hand on yours and we are kneading your breasts like bread dough together. I push them together and take one in my mouth and kiss it ever so gently, and then suck it into my mouth. I want your mouth on my shaft in the same way. He's hard and ready for you. He's released a pearl of liquid to share with you."

"I remember how you taste," I said. "Salty sweet. I love how you taste, especially after you have come inside me and our two juices have intermingled."

"I cannot contain him anymore," he said breathlessly. "I have to pull my pants down and release him or it will be painful. My shaft is so hard and long. Oh God, I want to fill you up."

"I'm using my fingertip to circle around my nub. It's so sensitive as I imagine you sucking on me, and it gives me a zing going right to my core."

"I can imagine how wet you are. I'm spreading wet around right now, pretending he's at your gates. I want to be inside you." He groaned deeply.

My breath caught as I dipped a couple of fingers into my opening, just to feel the same thing.

"My fingers aren't enough. Wait a sec, I'm getting something to play with, Rick," I said.

I picked up my bag and dug down into the bottom where I had a sex toy for emergencies. *Doesn't every girl carry one with her?* Turning it on, it buzzed gently. As I picked up my phone, I heard Rick gasp.

"I recognize that sound," he said. "It just sent a sizzle to my shaft. You have a sex toy."

"I do," I said. "I'm removing my panties now, so I can use it." I touched the vibrator to my already sensitive nub and the vibrations make me suck in my breath. As I moved it around, the tingles grew into a wave that threatened to crash over me.

"Oh God," I groaned. "This is going to climax me quickly."

"Insert it just a little, just the way I like to tease you," he said.

"I've already started," I said breathlessly. "It's not like you, too small, but it helps me imagine you inside me. I'm rubbing you on the inside and my coil is tightening."

"I'm imagining you close around me, squeezing me," he said. "You're so wet that I slide in easily."

"I'm pulling you out and holding you just at my gates. I'm imagining you getting impatient and wiggling," I said. I heard him utter little gasps and moans as his own hands simulated what I was telling him.

"I am pushing you in as far as possible," I said.

I thought of him filling me completely, the sensation of hitting the end of me and how the pain was a turn-on.

"I can hear your climax building," I said.

My breathing shortened to staccato groans and moans just like his. In fact, we were panting almost in rhythm.

"Ah, Lora, fuck me," came the whisper across the phone line.

"Ah, ah, ah, I have to pause," I said, almost climaxing. I nearly came, and didn't want this over so quickly.

I changed positions so I could simulate being on top. That let me get the most out of the toy. In this position, I could push the vibrator in farther—thank God it had a string—and moved back and forth on it as I would if Rick were under me.

"Rick, I'm on top now," I told him. "I've impaled myself on you as far as I can go. I'm slowly grinding my hips back and forth, stimulating my G-spot. I'm not going to last long this way."

I wanted to let go and make all the noise I wanted, but I couldn't do that. I needed to keep my mouth shut. It was difficult.

"I love the sounds you make," he said. His speech was slurred because of his arousal.

Staying connected, we heard each other's motion and the climax that was being built up. We were together on our tempo.

My groaning became keening as my climax took over. Rick matched me and as I let out a quiet scream; a quiet roar escaped him. We were both panting as we sat there for a few minutes together on the phone. Neither of us could speak for a few minutes.

"Well, that's some of the best self-gratification I've ever performed," chuckled Rick.

"It's always better with two," I answered. "But for the record, nothing compares. I'd much rather have been fucked hard by you any day of the week."

"I remember, you like it a little rough."

"I like a man who knows what he wants and how to take me, yes, wholly, without reservation, lay bare my soul," I answered with a thick voice.

I was aroused all over again just by the thought of us doing just that.

"I'll keep that in mind," he said, equally thick-voiced. "I appreciate a woman who knows what she likes and asks for it."

A calm came over me as my body sighed in happiness.

"Um, what now?" asked Rick.

"I am going to clean up my toy and myself and go back to work. I will call you later about New Year's, okay?"

"I'll be waiting," he said. "Oh, why do you have a toy at work?"

A small giggle escaped me. "Ah, I carry one with me in my bag, all the time," I said.

"Hmmm, really?" he asked. "Any particular reason?"

"Well, that is a long story. I will tell you the next time we see each other in person."

"Great, now I won't be able to focus on the desserts for tonight."

"Bye," I said in a sing-songy voice. I wasn't going to get that phone call out of my head, ever. I wasn't a prude, but I'd never had better phone sex.

It wasn't until nearly midnight that I could call him back. I had to put the kids to bed and shut down the house. In bed myself, I was ready for another sexy call if Rick wanted to play some more.

Rick answered the phone with a thick voice.

"By the time I got home," he said, "I was so horny I could barely walk. I couldn't stop thinking about you all day."

"Then I had the desired effect," I said. "Want to play some more?"

"Yes, I'm already in bed."

"So am I, and I put on some sexy lingerie for the occasion," I said. "Why don't we start off with a striptease?"

The groans of consent from Rick let me know it was playtime. Being each other's hands, we touched and aroused and played. I had brought some new toys too. We experienced their orgasms together again and again explosively.

"That was special," said Rick at the end.

"It's always better with two," I said. "Shall I bring my toys down with me?"

"Please, I want to try them out—I mean play with them—I mean play with you with them," he stammered. "Ah fuck, yes, please! I want to fuck you so much right now, I cannot think straight."

"Well, now that we have that cleared up," I chortled. "I'm looking forward to coming to Atlanta again."

"I'm looking forward to you coming too," he said.

Laughing hysterically, I said goodbye and hung up.

He's a keeper! I thought to myself.

Chapter 3

— Lora

"Lora, don't worry," said Armand. "I'm here."

"That's not the point, he was supposed to be here last night!" I screeched. "I have to get to the airport, and I have no idea where he is."

I was pacing now. All the luggage was at the front door, the kids were antsy, and being bratty because they were bored and didn't want to just wait. They wanted to go play. Meanwhile, it was 11:15, and I had to leave to get to the airport.

"He called and said he should be here to be here thirty minutes ago. He's always screwing up my schedule! I have a 1:00 flight, and I still need to be at the airport to do the check-in. I'm tired of always running because of being short of time."

"Do you want me to call him now?" asked Armand.

"I'm just grateful you're here. Thanks."

"Look, I'm here to cover for you if he doesn't show up."

"I am never sure about their father," I said. "He is in the running to be the least responsible person on the planet."

"Go! Your taxi is here," said Armand. "I'll handle it."

The taxi honked outside. My bags were already outside at the front door. I was so excited about this trip, it was going to be more like a vacation because I'd have more time down there. I'd gone on trips with girlfriends, and once with an ex, but never like this. This would be a whole week in paradise with a man I couldn't keep my hands off.

Oh my! I better go over what I've packed:

Evening wear, check. Lingerie, check. Casual, check. Bathing suit, check. Toys, check. Toiletries, check. Anything else? I don't think so, and if I missed anything I'll go shopping down there.

"Lora, GO!" yelled Armand. "Out of your reverie and get to the cab!"

Armand helped me to the curb with my bags. I gave him the details of where I was going to be staying and phone numbers.

"What time was Bruce supposed to be here?" he asked.

"He should have been here nearly an hour ago."

"Well, don't worry, I'll wait until he gets here and make sure they are going where they are supposed to go. But what if he doesn't show?"

"Hun, you have my permission to kill him if he doesn't show up," I said. "On second thought, don't. I won't get support from him if you do."

"No, really, Lora, what do I do?" asked Armand again.

"You have his number, give him a call and ask the bastard where he is and why he isn't there. Can you cover the kids until then? If you can't, I can't leave. And I'll understand," I said regretfully.

"No, go. I'll take care of it—whatever it is," he said. "Go have fun, I'll be here alone with nothing to do. I have no plans, so if worse comes to worst, I can watch them the whole week. But you'll owe me, Lora."

"Big time," I agreed. Kissing Armand on both cheeks, I launched myself into the taxi's back seat and told the driver to step on it. It was a fifteen-minute drive to the airport, and it was already 12:10. It was going to be yet another tight run to get to the plane. The taxi dropped me off at 12:23, which gave me thirty minutes to get checked in and to the gate.

God, I hate running for planes. I've really got to look into a spell to pause time!

Making it to the airport in record time, a worker was waiting to help me out of the car and to the gate with my luggage. At times like these, paying for assistance was not a problem.

I looked like a kid doing the pee-pee dance in the security line, because I was hopping up and down impatiently. My plane had just been called and I had three people in front of me.

"Excuse me! That was my flight that was just called. May I please cut the line?" I called to the security guard.

Motioning me ahead, I got dirty looks from some of the other passengers. *They can eat my dust! They don't have an ex who is always late picking up the kids.*

Getting through security, a guard called over a worker in a golf cart. They drove me to the gate! *Oh joy, I don't have to run for it!*

The driver radioed to the gate that he was bringing a late passenger.

At 12:57, they announced the last call for the flight. So, when we got to the gate, the airline people were waiting for me to close up the entrance. The driver called out, "Halt! Last passenger here was held up at security!"

Thankfully, the airline staff helped me grab my carry-on and get through the gate. I just hate getting to my seat on a plane all sweaty.

At least the flight appeared not to be full; the row I was in was empty except for me. I had one minute to get settled into my seat, so I didn't dally. Storing my carry-on above, I jumped into my seat, luckily by the window, and buckled in.

Happiness is an uneventful flight, and this was a happy flight. Landing in Atlanta was uneventful too, but finding my way through the crowds was a pain. The last time I came into Atlanta was late at night and the airport wasn't this busy. I had to go through customs first, so that was a long, roundabout way of leaving. Once I came through the cleared area, there was a crowd of welcomers waiting for people returning. Since I didn't expect anyone, I was walking right past the crowd toward the carousel.

And there he was, waiting for me, leaning up against a pillar.

Oh my, he is handsome!

I'd forgotten, sort of. Well, not forgotten, but the details weren't as sharp. Looking at him now, my libido went off the charts. He hadn't seen me yet, so I indulged myself and stared. His fine form; Y-shaped torso, with wide muscled shoulders, narrow waist and hips. I was such a sucker for Latinos. I adored his bronze skin and Latin looks. His chest was visible under the tight t-shirt he was wearing. And that ass, *growl*, was wonderfully covered in tight black jeans. I wanted to squeeze that ass.

His beautiful face was framed with long-ish, thick, black, satin-looking hair that set off the high cheekbones and deep-set, copper-coloured eyes. He had a strong chin and a Roman nose, giving him a perfect profile.

He had strong, yet finely shaped hands and fingers. I knew they were strong because I'd been on the receiving end of their kneading. Another growl escaped my throat.

Those long legs, muscled and straight, matched his long, strong arms. I remembered those arms wrapped around me and those legs holding me down. Another growl escaped, this time a little louder. A guy next to me glanced at me with a smile.

Not about you, buddy, I thought.

Swallowing the rising heat, I exited the arrivals area and called out to him with a wave of my hand.

"Lora!" he shouted back. Rick was waving his arms so I could see him. What a sweet man!

"Rick!" I called back. "I'm so happy to see you!"

We connected at the end of the gauntlet and he gave me a huge hug, picking me up off my feet and swinging me around.

"Weeeee!" I screamed. "Put me down, you big oaf, before I throw up!"

Laughing, he put me down but didn't let me go. Looking into my eyes, he was smiling a huge smile.

"You're a sight for sore eyes!" he exclaimed. "I couldn't wait to see you, so I thought I would surprise you here. I checked to see if the flights from Montreal were on time, and decided to take a chance."

"It is a very nice surprise, and a very welcome one. Thank you!" I hugged him again. He hugged me back, and the transfer of energy was electrifying. I hadn't noticed that before. Maybe it was due to emotions. *I'll have to watch that.* The only other person I got power readings on was Mark—well, now Falon too.

"Where is your luggage?" he asked me while releasing me a little, but not completely.

"I have to go to carousel six to get my suitcases. I have only two, though, and my carry-ons," I answered.

Rick led me over to carousel six, leaving me to stand and watch while he went looking for a cart. The luggage hadn't started to come around yet, so everyone was lining up. My luggage was purple, so it was easily identifiable.

Rick came back with the cart and stood behind me with his arms wrapped around my shoulders. The height difference between us was significant when I was wearing flats, as I was now. I barely came up to his armpit.

"I'm so happy you came down!" he started. "This New Year's will be so special."

"I'm happy to be here. It was a rush getting to the plane though. Bruce was late picking up the kids—again! I had to leave a friend there waiting for me. I hope that moron actually remembers he was to have the children for a week!" I said, getting angry all over again.

"Whoa! Forget the idiot, you're here with me. I want you to be prepared for being spoiled and pampered, and to let go of all the stress," he said, hugging me again.

"Sorry, yes, you're right, I've got to let it go," I agreed. "So what first?"

His eyes lit up and he looked at me with a huge smile.

"Well, to go back to my place, unpack, relax by the pool, sip some margaritas or whatever your poison is, and take in the South!"

"Oh, that sounds heavenly. Oh! There's my first bag!" I said, pointing to the purple bag that was rocking its way down the ramp and tilting out of the carousel. Rick reached over and grabbed it efficiently and lobbed it onto the cart. The second bag was right behind it, so I was going to jump for it, but Rick got there first and it was on the cart in a blink.

"Wow! That was easy!" I said.

"But of course! Come with me, my lady!" Rick said with flourish. Taking my arm and pulling it through his, he grabbed the cart and led us out of the airport to the parking lot. It was a long walk to find his car, his red Miata. Lucky for me, Mazdas had a lot of room in their trunks; all my bags fit in there. Without a back seat, it would have been "juggling on my lap" time.

The drive from the airport to his house south of Atlanta was fun. Rick put the top down and we drove along the highway with our hair blowing in the wind. What freedom!

His neighborhood was pretty swanky and the house was very large. Clearly, he was right. This man had money, something I found about him on the last trip down. I knew he had a successful restaurant business with a partner, but he must be really successful to have this house. My body remembered the last time I had done this drive. It was becoming stimulated as if I hadn't been laid in months. *Wait, it had been months. No wonder my hooha was hungry.* I reached over and put my hand on his leg as he was driving. Rick glanced at me and moved my hand closer to his body.

I moved my hand right up to his cock, and took my baby finger and gently started scratching on the outside of his jeans, which had become oh-so-tight again.

Rick groaned for me, and glanced at me again.

"Lora, if you keep doing that, I'll have to pull over before we get home," he said with a throaty voice.

"No you won't," I said. "You are not going to delay us from getting home, because I want you very badly." I continued to stimulate him with my finger.

He grabbed my hand as it was playing, and pushed it against his swelling cock. And then placed his hand back on the wheel.

"Does that mean you'd like me to play some more?" I asked, flirting with him.

"Please," he croaked out.

So I obliged him.

By the time we got back to his house, we were both ready to explode. So, he carried me from the car inside and right upstairs to his room.

His bedroom was the only room on the second floor. It had a view and direct access to the back yard. The focal point of the room was the colonial, four-poster bed with huge posts supporting a canopy of silk that draped all around the bed. *How romantic!* The first time I saw that bed, I got ideas in my head. I must have blushed, because Rick had glanced at me and smiled knowingly. Since then, we'd tried out the naughty idea that I had, and the bed was perfect.

"*Mamacita*, I'm so glad you're here," he murmured into my hair as he laid me down and joined me on the big king-sized bed.

"I'm very glad to be here," I said. "What does mamacita mean?"

"It means 'sexy lady,' but one that means something special to me." Rick walked to the bedroom door and called out: "Mama Anita, I'm back! Please get the front door for me? I'll get the luggage later." He closed the door and returned to me.

"Who is Mama Anita?" I asked.

"She's my housekeeper, but she has been with my family since I was a boy, so she's like a second mother to me. Decades ago, I started calling her "mama" and it kind of stuck.

"Ricardo, do you want me to bring dinner up to the room?" asked Mama.

"No, Mama, we'll come down and I'll properly introduce you, but for now I want Lora all to myself," said Rick, looking at me with heat in his eyes.

"First, I need to ravish you," he said, turning to me.

"Mmmm, ravish away, please."

He did. Rick knew exactly how I liked it: edgy and a little rough. During our first weekend together in October, we discovered we were very compatible sexually. He liked to dabble a bit, and I was a willing partner. I wasn't afraid to try things, and he was a very considerate lover, always making sure I was safe, comfortable, and okay with whatever we tried.

It was around midnight and we were cuddling, quiet, satisfied, but still awake.

"Why don't we go for a midnight swim?" he asked suddenly. "It's my favorite time of day to swim."

"Okay, let me get into a suit."

"There's no need," he said. "We'll be alone."

"Well, just a robe, then, in case we run into your Mama Anita."

"I'll meet you downstairs."

The pool was one of those fancy pools you see on HGTV. It was themed like a Caribbean island. It had a big slide made of natural rock and waterfall with a grotto, and an infinity edge pool off one end that looked over a small valley. There was even a beach entry in one corner. On the opposite end from that was a diving board, indicating a deeper end. Between the house and the pool was a beautiful deck and a built-in hot tub that had water cascading into the pool. I believe there were underwater seats up against the side to let you sit in the water while sipping drinks. And the water! It looked like the ocean in the Caribbean—it was that beautiful turquoise color. So inviting! The whole place was light up with spot lights accenting various points around the property, turning it into a very magical place.

The midnight swim was the final ingredient to get me relaxed, especially after such amazing sex. But I was soon starting to get sleepy, and we returned to his room and I slept soundly, until I heard the door open.

I rolled over and was lying on the bed, stretched out like a starfish, just relishing in the softness of the satin sheets, when Rick returned carrying a tray with coffee and pastries.

"I guess we missed dinner?" I asked.

"Yes, but Mama had some pastries set aside for us when we got hungry."

We sat in silence sipping the delicious coffee and nibbling on the excellent pastries. It was a major perk of dating a pastry chef.

"Let's eat on the deck."

That was a mild-mannered statement. It wasn't a deck like I had. This house was a mansion and it was appointed as such. When I was here last October, Rick had given me the whole tour.

It was a sprawling multi-level design with a big circular driveway leading to a three-car garage, and a large fountain in the middle of the circular drive. The front entrance had extra-wide, dramatic, double doors leading into a wide lobby. There was no other way to describe it. It wasn't a hallway; it was too big. It had double-high ceilings, and a grand circular staircase going up to some rooms. The whole floor was covered with intricately designed tiles.

"Rick, do these designs mean something?" I asked, admiring the floor.

"Si, these are traditional patterns from Mexico, my grandmother's country. They are cement tiles, and there is a traditional way of adding pigments to the tiles as the cement is setting using molds. Once the pigments are placed, the tiles are pressed, impregnating the cement with the color. It needs to cure for a couple of weeks."

"Wow, the colors are beautiful!"

"These floors can last a hundred years without cracking. In fact, in some places in Cuba, they're the last thing left in some of the old mansions."

There was a five-foot diameter table in the lobby with a huge vase of freshly cut flowers. The aroma was heavenly—like being in a botanical garden.

Beyond the lobby, was an open space lined with glass across the back of the house. You could see right through the house to the back yard, where there was an amazing pool. I walked that way first to get a look.

Attached to the house outside was a large outdoor kitchen and bar. There was a complete set of cooking appliances, ovens, barbeques, smokers, a pizza oven, and an outdoor fridge and sink with prep area. You could live out here all year round!

I think my jaw dropped to my chest at the fanciness of it all. Rick came up behind me, wrapped his arms around me, and put his head on top of mine.

"So what do you think? Are these accommodations sufficient?" he had asked.

"Your house is beautiful, Rick. I'm going to enjoy that pool!"

Sitting on said deck, we finished our coffee and pastries. In the bright morning light, I looked around and saw that the chaise lounges near the hot tub were set up.

"I had forgotten how magnificent this was," I said, teasing him. "We don't even have a public pool like this. My kids would go gaga over this."

"I think we used almost every corner the last time you were here," he said. "But of course we didn't really *use* the facilities."

He paused a moment, thinking, then said, "When you're comfortable, I would love to have your kids down here too. I've got lots of bedrooms. They can each have one, and we'll still be private in our own little world."

That was music to my ears, but I had to play it very close to the vest when my kids were concerned. I didn't mind taking chances with my heart, but theirs were a different matter altogether. I had to be pretty solid with a guy to introduce him into their lives. Rick had potential, but we weren't quite there yet. Still, it was so nice to dream.

"That would be nice," I answered cautiously. "While that topic has come up, we may as well talk about it."

"Okay," he said, looking a little nervously. "Let's get comfortable and then we can talk."

"Mama Anita!" he called out.

A rotund, happy-looking woman came out of the kitchen to my right. She approached me with a smile on her face, but her eyes showed love toward Rick.

"*Buenos Dias Ricardo,*" she answered.

"Good morning, Mama. I'm remiss in introducing you properly. Mama Anita, this is Lora, the amazing woman from Canada I was telling you about. Mama wasn't here the last time you were. It was her weekend off."

"Lora, it is a very great pleasure to meet you. My Ricki has been talking about you for months!" she said.

"Lora, this is my Mama Anita. She is my housekeeper and general life-keeper. If it weren't for her, I wouldn't be where I am today."

"You're too kind, Ricardo," replied Mama Anita. "I have been with his family since he was a young *chico.*"

"Anything you want, ask Mama for it," said Rick.

"Oh, I don't know about that," I said. "I don't have staff, so I wouldn't feel comfortable asking you for anything. I'm not used to that."

"Chica, is what I'm here for. Please let me do my job," said Mama Anita.

"I'll try," I said.

"Mama, could we please have some breakfast on deck? I brought the bags in too, so when you have a moment, please take them up to my room?" asked Rick.

"Si, Ricardo," she answered.

"Come with me, my darling. Let me show you the deck."

He drew my hand with him and led me outside. I hadn't expected it to be cold, but I was unprepared for the heat. It was like midsummer for me outside, even early in the morning. The moon still shone on one side of the sky, while the sun was casting long shadows across the deck. Light dancing across the movement of the water in the pool, it reflected wonderful waves of light on the surrounding building and structures.

"Oh, Rick, this is truly lovely," I said, choosing one of the loungers. Its cushions were soft and comfy. "I could get used to this life!"

"It's an option for the future," he said.

Mama Anita came outside with two tall coffees, plus some fresh fruit, rolls, and butter.

"This is perfect!" I said, taking one of the coffees and sipping it. Nibbling on the fruits and fresh breads, I felt like I was a queen. I hadn't realized how hungry I was!

"So let's talk about your kids?" asked Rick, diving in.

"Well, first, just about my philosophy on dating," I started. "I wanted to let you know I have some ground rules. I want us on the same page before we go any further. I like knowing where I stand with people."

"Very wise. I like that you are direct," said Rick.

"Okay. Here goes. My kids are everything to me. I protect them from all the crap in my life and I don't expose them to men, lovers, boyfriends, or any significant others, unless I feel that the relationship is stable and has a future. That hasn't happened yet. I let my lovers know about my kids, but my kids remain oblivious until I know the relationship is solid."

"I completely agree with that," he answered me. "I too have children, although they are grownups and live on their own. But that is the way I would have it and no other. What we do as adults doesn't need to up-heave their world and cause them chaos."

A mature man who seems to agree with me. Wow!

I'm thinking that way a lot today.

"I'm very glad you agree with me, because that's a showstopper for me. We had a fun time together and it was just a singles thing back then, but this is different for me. This isn't just a date, and it isn't just a fun weekend hooking up. To me there is more on the line. Does that make sense?"

"It does," he said. "This week means more to me as well. When we hooked up for the Miami trip, it was a surprise how compatible we were, how well we fit, emotionally, intellectually, and sexually. That hasn't happened since my last wife. Then in October, we discovered more about each other, and it just keeps getting better for me."

"Your wife?"

"Yes, she passed away about seven years ago," he explained. "When she died, I was devastated, and never thought I would have another relationship. However, since October, I must admit I've sort of been consumed by thoughts of you. This is rare for me," he admitted. "I didn't know what to do with my feelings. It was Mama Anita who told me to call the girl."

I smirked. "Call the girl, go on and call the girl," I sang in the melody from *The Little Mermaid*. "I remember that scene with the lobster. It seemed appropriate."

Laughing and picking up the melody, Rick continued the song, substituting words to fit his situation. By the time he was finished, we were both laughing until tears were leaking from our eyes. Mama Anita had come out to see what the noise was all about. When she saw Rick singing and dancing the lobster song, she shook her head and returned to the house, laughing. Strains of *"Kiss de girl, go on and kiss de girl,"* were coming out the kitchen window.

"Lora, you don't have to worry about me rushing things," said Rick earnestly. "I promise, every step of the way it will be both of us deciding to take the next step. I have no expectations here. I only wanted you with me because, well, frankly, my life felt empty without you here."

"You're such a sweet man, Rick," I said with tears in my eyes for a different reason. "How did I ever get lucky enough to meet you?"

"Blame Falon," he said, laughing. "It's her fault."

"Ah, Falon. Yes, she and I have got in and out of many scrapes together!"

"There's a story or two there, I think?" he asked.

"We've lots of time to explore those."

"Indeed," he said. "So Falon and I almost were a hook-up."

"Really?"

"Fate intervened though. But I was drawn very strongly to her. You and she are quite similar, and yet very different."

"Yes, that's true," I said. "So tell me about this near hook-up."

"Of course."

Rick then told me his version of the story I had already heard from Falon, complete with his feelings throughout. Having heard the story once, it was a unique opportunity to be able to detect if he had a penchant for exaggeration or lying, and none of that happened. Interestingly, it was almost identical.

Honest, straightforward. Oh, Goddess, you've given me a true gift of a man. May I keep him, please?

The only difference in his story was a minimizing of how endowed he was and how far they had gotten. It was cute. He didn't want me to know that he had actually penetrated her when the phone rang. Or maybe he hadn't realized it? I don't know. I listened and laughed when he made light of it, and commiserated when he showed disappointment.

I could have been jealous, but that was not me. I don't really feel jealousy. I might have in this case, because he was quite smitten with Falon at first. But his description of how he felt when he met me the first time just banished that completely.

"The day I met you," he started, "it felt as though time stopped. All I could see was you. Your emerald-green eyes looked into my soul and laid me bare. From that moment I had to have you, body and soul. Getting to make love to you had a profound effect on me and was an amazing climax to that weekend."

"I remember that day too," I reminisced. Oh, my heart strings were tugged on that score. "I had just arrived at the airport and you, Mark, and Falon picked me up and then we were racing down the highway to Miami. My first reaction to seeing you two guys was: Oh my God, they're gorgeous! Falon laughed when she thought I meant the two cars," I said, chuckling.

"That weekend was spectacular from the ride down, to the award dinner, to the dancing, to the lovemaking, and especially getting to know you," he said quietly. "I especially liked talking and getting to know you."

"Me too," I said. "I so rarely talk with adults, especially men. It was a breath of fresh air to have a man just comfortable talking about anything."

"Now that we have had this trip down memory lane, what would you like to do next?" he asked.

"Can we just sit here—holding hands perhaps—and just be?" I asked hopefully. I didn't really want to do anything but enjoy the night, the moon, the atmosphere, and most importantly, his company.

"That sounds perfect to me," he agreed. "Let's just be." He got up then and pushed the two chaises together and locked them. So now it was one chaise and we could lie in each other's arms, listening to the night birds and crickets.

It was perfect.

Chapter 4

— Falon

It has been a strange four months, thought Falon. *It happened. It really happened. But that was last August.*

A week after the bite, Mark made a small cut in my hand, which bled like a stuck pig. But before my eyes the bleeding slowed and eventually stopped. I watched as the slice in my hand knit itself back together. It was freaky. After ten minutes, there was no evidence left that he had done anything.

"Good, your body is responding to the venom," said Mark.

"That was freaky to watch," I said.

"The first time, it was unsettling. But it will go faster the more your body adapts."

"How fast?"

"It should heal most minor wounds almost instantly. More complex wounds take a little while. Grave injuries take weeks."

"What's a grave injury?" I asked, not really wanting to know.

"Loss of a limb, or something equally as severe."

Shuddering, I said, "What can't you heal from?"

"Mortal wounds for us include decapitation or our heart removed."

"Got it. Can't grow another head," I said in jest.

Could it be that I'm really immortal now? I still don't feel different. Then again, I'm not doing anything different yet.

I expected more signs that things were changing, but the only thing I got was feeling like I had the flu. My body ached for weeks; I had a fever and I couldn't keep food down. Mark told me the aches were my body remaking itself, strengthening the bones and skeleton. It was the same as growing pains as teens get. As long as I had a fever, it indicated that my body was fighting the venom's work.

Once the "non-flu" passed, I suddenly had more energy and stamina for things, and I was starving. My appetite was huge and I was experiencing cravings I hadn't had before, like a craving for meat.

This New Year's Eve, Lora went down to Atlanta to be with Rick. So we wouldn't be reveling together. However, that was wonderful, because I really thought those two had something special together. They were such a strong pairing—just like Mark and I. Lora and I had talked several times since they hooked-up in Miami and her subsequent weekend in October.

I think she's fallen for him completely.

She even used her witch powers to get a read on him and discovered there was something different about him. Lora only used magic on guys she was interested in more than just a hook-up. Most didn't make the cut. Rick did though, on all accounts.

Lora had talked about a connection she felt from him, something similar to what she felt from Mark, and now myself. She explained it as a power connection. She had one with Mark when she first met him. She had done the Origin spell on Mark and discovered his origins were not human. She knew right then that he was very special. Rick gave her the same feelings, only stronger. Her intention was to perform the same spell on him.

Wouldn't it be awesome if Rick were another Olde One? I mean, would Mark know if there was another branch of his family? Is there more than one family?

Mark and I didn't have plans for New Year's Eve. We intended to spend a quiet night at home watching movies. I'd never really been one to go out and get drunk on New Year's, and it was just nice to be at home with Mark.

"Hey, hon, where is the cheese we got yesterday?" asked Mark from the kitchen. He was putting together a wine and cheese night for us, complete with finger food and treats. I was looking forward to it. "They're all in the bottom drawer of the fridge because I had no room in the cheese compartment," I answered.

Ten minutes later, he came out with a delectable tray of cheeses and laid them on the dining room table, then went back for a few different bottles of wine to go with the cheeses. It was quite the spread.

"Hey, Mark, are there any other families of Olde Ones?" I asked.

"Hmmm." He paused. "I am not sure. Why do you ask?"

"I was just thinking of Lora and what she had said about Rick being special and having some sort of power connection," I said. "She wants to do another spell to see if she can learn more about him like she did about you."

"Gwen may know. I'm not aware of others. Our family is only about 150 people or so. I wouldn't be surprised if there were others," said Mark.

"I wonder how the preparations are going for the New Year's Eve bash in Atlanta?" I asked.

"Knowing Rick, they are going to be spectacular," said Mark.

Chapter 5

— Lora

Justin and Rick had decided the theme for the party for New Year's Eve was *A Night of Stars*. They were planning on decking out the restaurant with all kinds of twinkling lights on the ceilings, which were twelve feet high, and create cool effects with fog machines. The invitations that had been sent out said:

YOU'RE INVITED TO OUR

NEW YEAR'S EVE CELEBRATION

A NIGHT OF STARS

THERE WILL BE TWO SITTINGS: 6:00 AND 10:00

PLEASE RSVP BY DECEMBER 20TH

After a day of glorious rest and relaxation with Rick, the big day had arrived. I had settled in very nicely. I loved the pool in the backyard.

Rick was all business that morning, on the phone with a host of people making sure everyone was where they were supposed to be. The restaurant was expecting five hundred dinner guests in two sittings tonight.

The first sitting was an early dinner at 6:00 p.m.; those guests would be out by 9:00 p.m. The first sitting was just dinner and dancing. It catered to the older crowd that had no interest in staying up to ring in the New Year. Some of those clients also went to private parties or a bar at midnight.

The second sitting was at 10:00 and it was the midnight special one. Those guests would be getting dinner, dancing, then midnight dessert. Since there were two serving sessions, Rick needed to make sure the restaurant had enough servers who were staying late.

By noon, Rick was already at the restaurant organizing the chefs and getting the cooking started. All the entrees had to be in the oven cooking before 2:00 to make sure they were all ready. Then another wave of entrees needed to be prepped and ready for the ovens at 6:00 to go in as soon as the first round came out.

The dessert ovens were going double-time. Because most of the desserts were cold served, just about everything was being prepared in advance. The kitchen staff were jumping.

I was left at the house to get ready. Rick said he would be back by 8:00 to change into his evening clothes and bring me to the restaurant. He had reserved a table for us at the 10:00 sitting. Justin was the chef on duty for the second sitting. Rick was the chef on duty for the first sitting. It was good that they could work like that.

I had planned on wearing the same dress I wore last August to the award dinner, but Rick had surprised me with a new designer gown in emerald-green satin that was to die for. It was a strapless gown with a sweetheart neckline and a plunging back. The dress skirt had two layers. The outer layer split down the front in flowing waves of satin. The outer layer came off to reveal a curve-hugging short dress underneath that was easy to dance in.

Since this dress meant I needed to go shopping for undergarments, I decided I would get my hair and nails done too. I went to Saks and found a stunning lacy bra in green, and matching thong to match the dress—what luck. I walked down to the cosmetics department, found my favorite counter, and asked for a beautician to do my makeup for the evening.

"What a striking face to work with," said the beautician.

"Thank you," I answered. Showing her the underwear, I told her the dress was the same color.

"It will match your eyes perfectly. We need to make them dramatic," she said. "How about some jewels to accentuate those beautiful features?"

"Sure, why not," I answered.

The beautician took about an hour to do my full makeup. When she was finished, she packed some jewels in a small bag.

"Here are some jewels that the hairdresser can use in your hair too," she said.

"Thank you."

The result was pretty special. I looked like a supermodel. Next stop was the salon for hair and nails.

The hair designer came up with a swept-up coif that intricately wove a coil of hair into elaborate Celtic knots—he chose this once he learned I was Irish and was wearing green—and glued the gems into my hair to enhance the knots. Dropped ringlets surrounding my face gave me a soft look that was so sexy and very elegant.

"Oh my God," said the hair designer. "Girl, you are stunning!"

"You've done splendid work," I said. "I especially love the ringlets. It leaves it looking less severe than having it all up."

"Girl, if I wasn't into men, I'd have a hard-on looking at you!" he giggled.

The whole effect was absolutely stunning. I had never felt so beautiful.

I can't believe that is me! I thought, admiring the work in the mirror. *Rick isn't going to know what hit him.*

Looking at my nails for the first time, I was stunned to see exquisite green polish and white rhinestone designs on very long nails.

Glancing at the time, I saw that I needed to get back to the house.

"Can you please call me a cab? I have to skedaddle," I said.

"One's on its way, five minutes," said the receptionist.

Gathering all my things while trying to not mess up my beautiful nails that the esthetician had done was not easy.

Once home, checking the clock, I had two hours to finish getting ready. Should be plenty.

Laying out the clothes on the bed, I drew a bath for myself just to freshen up. While I was catching a second in the tub, Mama Anita knocked on the door.

"Miss Lora, would you like some help getting ready?" she asked.

"Oh, Mama Anita, that would be lovely, thank you. I will call you when I need help getting into my dress."

"Si, Miss, I wait."

I rinsed off and got out of the tub. Toweling dry with a big thirsty bath towel was another luxury I wasn't used to. Checking my hair and makeup, I was good. Maybe I only needed to fix the back of my hair a bit.

Dropping the towel over the tub, I went into the bedroom to find Mama Anita waiting patiently.

"Oh, Miss, your hair is *magnifico*! I will help you fix the back though, 'cause the curls have dropped in the water. Here, get into your underwear and I'll get the iron."

Not used to having a "mom" taking care of me, I almost felt affronted, but set it aside. It was coming from a place of love and I should get over myself. So I got myself into the new bra and thong. I wasn't wearing stockings because it was too hot down here.

Mama Anita came back with a curling iron and a chair.

"Sit, sit, I'll fix your hair," she directed me.

Sure enough, with deft fingers she made quick work of repairing the tiny amount of damage the wind and the tub had done to the sculpture that was my hair.

"Miss, wait, I have something for you to wear." She ran out of the room and was back a minute later with a box.

"This was Ricardo's mama's. She wore it on their wedding day," said the housekeeper. "It would go perfectly with this dress."

She opened the box to show me a necklace and earring set in emeralds and diamonds. The emeralds were square cut with tiny diamonds around them and strung in a short row of ten. It was almost a choker but lay flat on my chest at the bottom of my neck. The earrings were two more of the emerald/diamond settings as studs. They twinkled beautifully under my hair.

"Oh my God, I feel like a princess!" I said, starting to tear up.

"Oh, don't do that, you'll smudge that beautiful makeup!" cried Mama Anita. "Ricardo's mama would love you in this. Green was her favorite color. Let's get you into that dress!"

Together, we got me into the dress and securely taped it in. The lace bra was just visible above the neckline of the dress, adding femininity and sexiness. The open back plunged down to my waist. The outer layer of the skirt hooked on nicely and seemed secure. Mama Anita showed me that I could use the long skirt as a cape if I got cool coming home. Brilliant idea.

"All I need are the shoes," I said, getting the black stilettos from the box. They had green and diamond rhinestones in a pretty design on the outside and top edge. It all coordinated—amazing.

I stood in front of the floor-to-ceiling mirrors and assessed my image. I'd never been dressed up like this before. I'd dressed up, but compared to this it had been tawdry and cheap looking. This was elegance personified and it was sexy as hell. Couldn't get much better.

"Miss Lora, you are a vision," said Mama Anita, gazing in the mirror with me.

"Thank you, Mama Anita," I answered. I smiled with the moniker I used. I think she liked being mama to everyone. "Your help was invaluable."

"Honey, I'm home!" rang out Rick from downstairs.

"Oh! Stay there for a moment, will you?" I asked.

"Okay?"

"Go on, show him!" said Mama.

I walked out of the bedroom to the top of the circular stairs leading down to the lobby. Rick wasn't looking up yet—he was looking out the back doors.

"Ahem," I said quietly.

He looked up at me and his jaw dropped. I smiled. He stood there and stared like I don't know what—mesmerized. It took a few minutes until he realized he hadn't said anything. By that time I had started to descend the stairs. I stopped on the second last step and waited.

"*Ah mon Dios!*" he breathed out. "Lora, you are the most beautiful vision I have ever seen. You rival the Goddess Aphrodite. I am your humble servant." He bowed low.

I stepped down to the floor, and gently swatted his shoulder with my hand.

"I don't want a servant, humble or otherwise. You like?" I asked, doing a little spin for him. "Who is this goddess you've been hanging out with?"

"Lora, I love—uh, love what you're wearing. How am I going to not ravish you all night long? I see Mama has brought you my mama's jewels. That is good. It's a shame that they hide in a safe all the time. They were meant to be worn by a woman of beauty such as yourself."

I was blushing now, which was new for me. Not much made me self-conscious.

"It's the dress. You have exquisite taste, Rick," I added.

"Ah, that was easy as pie," he said. "I simply had to match your eyes. As soon as I saw that dress, I knew it was made for you. I was right too. I am so sad that your makeup is so perfect though."

"Why?" I asked, confused.

"Because I can't kiss those luscious lips!" he answered. "They're begging to be kissed. *Ah mon Dios!* I'm not going to make it through this evening."

Shaking his head, he scooted around me and went upstairs to get ready for the evening. I watched him go and smiled. I'd never been in a position like this before, driving a man wild with anticipation by just standing still.

The night is going to be interesting.

"Rick, do I need to carry a purse?" I asked.

"No, love, you don't need to carry anything unless you want to," he said. "If you want, I can put your lipstick in a pocket for you so you have nothing to carry."

Hmmm, that was a good offer, because it would have been put down my cleavage otherwise.

"Okay, deal. I won't bring anything but lipstick. That way these luscious lips will remain cherry red for you all night."

It's a good thing I purchased all the makeup the beautician used on my face!

Thirty minutes later, Rick came downstairs in a tuxedo. He was wearing a wine-colored shirt with a black bowtie and a deep red rose in his lapel.

My, my, my, my, my, he looked delicious! Turnabout apparently was fair play.

He came running down the stairs and stopped in front of me where I was perched on a bar stool.

"How do I look? Good enough to accompany you?" he asked shyly.

"My dear man, you look good enough to eat," I answered.

His response to me was a smile dripping with suggestion and hooded eyes.

"We don't have to show up on time," he suggested in a voice that meant all sex and no business whatsoever.

"I cannot do my hair like this—so we're not messing it up yet!" I grinned at him. "But afterwards, I want you to mess me up everywhere, got it?"

Groaning, and adjusting himself a little in his tuxedo pants, he was still looking at me. Reaching out with a finger, he brushed the top of my dress where the lacy green bra was decorating my breast oh so lightly. It was a demi-tasse bra, and I'm a DD, so my nipples were sitting above the solid part of the bra peeking out from behind the lace. The dress was covering them, but it wouldn't take very much to expose me. He was licking his lips and teasing my nipples from outside my dress until they were standing up at attention.

That made me groan too. I leaned toward him as he took a step toward me. He pulled my dress down and peeled the lace below my nipple and took it between his lips. He gently sucked on it, and then sucked in as much as he could. The gasp that left my lips must have been heard upstairs by Mama.

"Stop that, or we'll never get out of here," I murmured. I didn't really want him to stop. It felt amazing. My body had become so sensitive to him, and so over-sexed since meeting Rick that I almost had an orgasm when he touched me.

He'd exposed my other breast, and while he was sucking on the first one his fingers were pinching and flicking the other.

"Rick, I'm all wet now. Are you happy?"

"Oh, Lora, I'm beyond happy. But now I need to fuck you something bad."

I pushed him back a bit, got down from the stool, raised my dress above my hips, and swept the long part out of the way as I sat back down on the stool. When Rick saw what I was doing, he undid his belt and pants and let them fall to the floor.

He took my hips and slid my bottom to the front of the stool. He spread my legs and stepped between them. He moved my thong out of the way with one finger and in one smooth motion drove into me. That one act of ownership turned me on so much I almost climaxed.

Rick paused for a moment to let us feel the connection. Taking a breath, I swallowed my excitement, just in time for Rick to slam into me again, and again, and again.

"Ah, ah, AH ... *fuck*!" I screamed as my climax took me. Rick was right behind me as he slammed into me one last time and his seed exploded into me. As his cock was jerking the last of its payload, his head flopped against my shoulder.

We stayed there for a minute or so. I realized that the housekeeper could walk through this part of the house at any time.

"Rick, we have to separate," I urged gently, although my legs felt like wet spaghetti, and I wasn't sure I could even stand.

"Mmm, umm, yeah. Give me a minute until brain function returns," he murmured. "Lora, you have a way of bringing me on so hard I see stars. So much I have to fight this amazingly strong compulsion to bite you."

"I can't believe I came so quickly," I admitted. "But I haven't been with anyone else since you. Wait a minute, bite me?"

"You too?" he asked. "Neither have I, and I must admit, you are worth every second. At least now the sexual tension is broken for me, a little. I'll survive seeing you and being with you in this dress all night. I'll explain later about the bite."

Pulling out, he said, "Oh my God. That was wonderful. Wait here."

Picking up his trousers quickly, he ran into a washroom and came back a few seconds later with a cloth to clean us up. Once he had himself zipped up and restored to the elegant vision he was, he helped me down from the stool so that my dress wouldn't get stained.

"Will you be okay, or will you leak some more?" he asked.

"I better bring a towel in the car just in case," I answered with a grin. "Satin shows everything!" I shoved a towel between my legs so I could sit on it.

Arriving at the restaurant, I saw that the place was hopping. The first sitting was completely sold out and the revelers were all having a wonderful time. The band was playing some great music too, and that meant there were a few couples already up and dancing.

Justin spied Rick walking through the door and came over to us immediately.

"Oh, thank God you're here!" cried Justin.

"Why? What's happened?" asked Rick.

"Two of the servers didn't show up and I've been covering," he cried shrilly. "As a result I'm not in the kitchen supervising!"

"Okay, I'll help out with service, you go back and make sure everything is going the way it should. Was everything ready on time?" Rick asked.

"Yes, the prep was done perfectly, thank you. It's just getting those damned sous-chefs to work faster in getting the plates made up!"

"Go! I'll take over here. What's left to serve?" asked Rick.

"Just coffee and dessert to about twenty-five percent of the tables," answered Justin as he ran to the kitchen.

"Well, good thing we got here early, isn't it?" I said. "I know how to wait tables. Let me help."

"You cannot do that in those shoes, you'll kill yourself!" said Rick.

"Oh yeah? Just watch me!"

He didn't know I had lots of experience with serving tables in four-inch heels. I walked into the kitchen and grabbed the first plates ready, asking which table they were for. The seating arrangements were laid out clearly on the wall as you left the kitchen, so I easily located the correct tables. Walking out the door, I sashayed and swished my way around the tables and got to the correct ones and charmed the customers as I apologized for the delay. Dropping off my plates, I returned to the kitchen and got some more.

Rick watched for a moment, proud of me, in spite of having no right to be. He too ran into the kitchen and grabbed a few plates and delivered them. It didn't take very long to get everyone served.

After that, as a couple, and owner of the restaurant, we walked around to the tables and greeted everyone and asked how everything was going.

After they put out that fire, we went back to the kitchen to see what was happening. After all, we were going to be on duty for the next seating, and wanted to find out what happened to the missing servers.

"Rick, Lora, thank you so much for pitching in out there. You're both lifesavers!" cried Justin. He was an emotional man, but chefs are usually hot or cold.

"Don't think anything of it," I replied. "I've worked in the service industry. I understand how to smooth things over when there's a bump in the road. "

"You did much more than that," said Rick. "I was watching you. You're a natural hostess. You charmed everyone, including the women."

"You are a vision tonight, Lora!" complimented Justin. "I'm so glad you are here."

"So who didn't show up, Justin?" ask Risk.

"Melanie and Tiger," said Justin. They were two temporary servers that were hired on for the evening. Unfortunately, it's difficult to count on the temps. If they get a better offer somewhere else, they just duck out.

"Let me see if I can find some replacements for the second sitting," said Rick. Let's go to the office, Lora. We can work on this problem quietly. Is everything under control back here now, Justin?"

"Yes, the kitchen is under control now. Although, I think I'm going to stay for the night to make sure it *stays* under control. I'm going to let you guys take the front, I'll take the back."

"Sounds like a good idea," said Rick. "It was a dream that we could get through a big night like tonight with only one of us managing. But it's good to know. We have always worked best together."

"Right on, brother," agreed Justin.

Rick led me to the office behind the kitchen. It was down the same hallway where the storage room for dry goods was located. The walk-in fridge and freezer were back the other way. When we got to the office, I sat in one of the chairs while Rick went behind the desk and opened up a file with a list of people in it. I presumed they were all servers.

"Hello, is Charity there please?" asked Rick over speakerphone.

"Yes, may I ask who's calling?" said a female voice.

"It's Rick Benal from Escalata Restaurant."

"Just a moment please." A few moments later Charity came on the phone.

"Hey, Rick, what's up?" asked Charity.

"I've got a bit of an emergency. Are you available to wait tables for a late shift, 10-1? I'll make it worth your while," asked Rick.

"Sure, I didn't have anything planned tonight. My boyfriend is working. Is it black tie?"

"Yes, it is. Wait staff is all in black, trousers, and long sleeves. I have black ties at the restaurant if you need one, and black aprons too. You're a lifesaver. Two temps bailed on us."

"Oh God, I hate temps. They're always bailing. Sure, no problem. I like getting good tips! I'll be there by 9:30 for a briefing."

"Thank you. Bye," said Rick. "Well, that's one down, one to go."

Calling another name on the list, he repeated the same message.

"Hey, Rick, it's April. What can I do for you?"

"April, two of my temp servers bailed and I need another to fill their place for the second seating tonight. Are you available? I'll make it worth your while," asked Rick.

"For you, love, of course! Black tie? I'll be there by 9:30 for a briefing!" said April.

"Thank you, love!" said Rick. "Okay, that's solved. What's the next problem?"

"There has to be another problem?" I asked.

"No, but there usually is," he grinned. "Until then, we can smooch back here and no one will come and bother us—well, Justin would."

"Smooching sounds like a dangerous game to play when we may end up being public greeters," I reasoned.

"Hmm, you're right. How about a little?" he begged.

Walking around the desk, he leaned against the front and looked down at me.

"I have no right to say this but … when I was watching you take charge, my heart swelled with pride in knowing you. You are amazing, you know?"

"I've just been there. I understand what's at stake, and I like helping," I minimized the compliment. It didn't make me feel uncomfortable, but I felt it was undeserved.

"No, you are a professional," he said appreciatively. "No matter what you do, it is with grace and poise."

Shaking off the compliments, I stood and walked up to him and stood between his legs. Leaning against him, I wrapped my arms around his neck and looked deep into his eyes.

"Rick, I love that you appreciate me. I'm just doing what I would do for anyone because I have the skill. It's not a stretch. I like helping those I care about."

"Are you feeling this too? I feel so close to you. Like I've known you for years. I'm discovering I care about you much more than I thought was possible in so little time together."

"I think I am. I don't get it, but we have a connection, and it isn't mundane."

"We'll talk more about this tomorrow," Rick said. "Right now I just want to kiss you," he said, wrapping his arms around my waist. Dropping his mouth to mine, I tilted my head up to meet his. Our kiss was gentle, and yet it sent sparks right to my center. It felt like we were zapped by some force; his body instantly reacted and he grew hard.

"We can't do this much more here without me ripping this beautiful dress off and ravishing you," he murmured into my mouth.

"I agree. The closer I am to you, the more I want your body naked and on top of me. By the time we are finished tonight, I will need you to own me with everything you have. I want to be ravished by you." I pressed myself against him, grinding my hips against his cock and pushing hard into his mouth with my tongue.

"Rick!" came a call from down the hall.

Gasping for air, Rick pulled away.

"Yes?"

"Is it safe to come in? Or have you two started to shag yet?" asked Justin.

"We're still dressed and decent," answered Rick.

"Well, that's a shame!" said Justin walking into the office. "Listen, guys, thanks for getting everything under control. I really appreciate it. So thanks."

"I have called Charity and April," said Rick. "They're both very professional. I'm going to make it worth their while by doubling their base salary."

"That's fine with me. We're killing it tonight. The alcohol sales alone will pay for them," said Justin. "Listen, get out there and do your thing, Rick. The next wave will start showing up soon. I've got all the tables bussed and reset, but the reservations will be coming in early. We may as well get them drinking right away!"

"Consider it done!" said Rick. "My lady, would you please accompany me to the party?"

"Certainly, my lord, it would be my honor. Perhaps I can help as well instead of just standing around and doing nothing," I said.

"Girl, you can stand and be a statue and it would be gracing us with your presence. You look divine tonight!" exclaimed Justin. "But if you want to be a hostess, I'm not stopping you. It will only bring more glamor to our restaurant!"

"I want to see the reviews tomorrow for sure!" said Rick.

We went back out to the restaurant and discovered that the lights had been dropped, the tables were all reset—differently—done up with party favors, hats, and noisemakers. Each table had a bottle of champagne on ice too. It looked very festive and very pretty. The band was taking a one-hour break after playing until 9:00. They would come back on when people start being seated again.

Fifteen minutes later, Charity showed up for duty and April was right behind her, both on time and ready to work. By the front door there were two bar chairs for Rick and I to sit on between customers. That was a nice thing to do. The barkeeps were replacing empty bottles and making sure they had everything stocked again. Apparently they sold a lot of alcohol.

I took a seat beside the door as Rick was walking around and checking details on the tables. The two owners were perfectionists, which was why they were a success. People expected a lot out of their eateries, and reviews were nasty if anything went wrong, no matter how insignificant. The service industry really did get the brunt of rude behavior, especially when mixed with alcohol. It was the reason I had gotten out of it. I grew tired of being yelled at by drunk people. At least this environment was less likely to have rude people and more likely to have good tips. Sometimes good tips made the abuse worthwhile.

A young couple decked out in their finest walked through the door. Rick was in the back of the restaurant fixing details so I took over as hostess. "Good evening, and welcome to Escalata! Do you have a reservation tonight?"

"Yes, under Patisse, please."

I checked the seating plan that was left in place on the dais to find their table first. "You're at table 125. Right this way please." I escorted them to the table right near the dance floor. "Here you are. It is a fixed menu this evening, but can I get you beverages to start?"

"Yes please," said the customer. "My wife will have a margarita, and I would like a Macallan's. Neat please."

"Coming right up!" I walked to the bar and put the order in for table 125 and returned to the door. When I got there, Rick was there and speaking to some more customers. "You are at table 100," said Mark.

"I'll take them." Turning to the couple, I said, "Right this way please."

Also by the dance floor, the couple took their seats.

"The menu is fixed this evening, but can I get you some beverages to start?" I asked.

"Please, tequila neat, and scotch neat, don't care on brand," said the man.

"Very good. Thank you," I returned to the bar and put the order in for table one hundred. "Hey, is there a server ready to work the bar yet?" I asked.

"Yes, Charity is here. I'll call her up," said the bartender.

"Good, then I can be quicker in returning to the door."

"Do you work here?" asked the barkeep.

"No, just helping out tonight," I answered.

"Wow, you make a very classy hostess. It will make a huge difference to all of us. So thank you!"

Nodding in response, I walked back to the front door. There were now three couples waiting at the door. Rick was chatting up the next couple and welcoming them as one of the owners/chefs of the place. The couple was quite impressed that the owners were there at the door.

I picked up the couple and the table number and escorted them like a pro. Then I glanced over at Charity, who was waiting at the bar, to come and take the drink order, before returning for the next table.

It went like that for forty-five minutes solid as all the tables filled up. Everyone got drinks immediately, and by 10:15 the band had started playing too, so people were up and dancing already. At 10:30, the first course was coming out of the kitchen.

Rick and I took our own table by the kitchen doors and sat and waited for our food. We'd be served last, of course. But that gave Rick time to circulate and find out if everyone was having fun. During the night, we even got to dance a little. But I had the most fun being at his side as we hosted. It was such a positive experience getting to greet the customers and then speak to them during the evening.

Dinner service was finished by 11:30. The final course, dessert, was only going to come out after midnight. That gave the kitchen time to bus the tables and servers to open and pour the champagne. It also gave the guests time to dance and order new drinks.

Justin and Rick had a little show planned for midnight. Leaving me at the table, Rick went and got Justin from the kitchen, first making sure he was presentable. Justin had been clever; he'd removed his tuxedo jacket and shirt and put on an apron while working in the kitchen. So he quickly ducked into the office and got re-dressed. The two owners came out and went up on stage with five minutes to spare before midnight.

"Ladies and gentlemen!" Rick cried out on the mic. "If you could all take your seats for a moment, please. We have some door prizes for you this evening."

Waiting for everyone to return to their seats, Justin grabbed a top hat and was waving it around theatrically. He waved at me to come up on stage with them.

"Folks, we have three minutes to go before midnight. After the ball drops, we will be serving dessert with coffee or tea and liqueurs. You will find flutes of champagne served at your tables."

The New York New Year's Eve broadcast was turned on the big screen and everyone was watching. Rick motioned to Lora to join him on stage.

"Ten, nine, eight, seven, six, five, four, three, two, one! Happy New Year, everyone!" Justin and Rick yelled together! Everyone was screaming, hugging, kissing, and jumping up and down.

Rick and Justin hugged. Then Rick turned and took me up in his arms and delivered a big kiss on stage. He handed me a flute and we linked arms and sipped together.

"Ladies and gentlemen, please note your table number on the stand in the arrangement. This is the number we're going to call for the door prizes," said Justin. There was an excited murmur of voices as they all took their seats again.

Justin, being theatrical again, waved and bounced the top hat around and swept it before me. It was way above my eyes, so I couldn't see. I reached inside and pulled out a number and gave it to him.

"The first prize, a dinner for two valued at $250 here at Escalata, goes to—" pausing for effect— "table number 139!" cried Rick into the mic. Justin got me to draw another number.

A scream somewhere on the floor happened as someone jumped up and ran to the stage. Justin presented her with the certificate and shook her hand.

"The second prize, another dinner for two valued at $250 here at Escalata, goes to—" pausing again "—table number 101!" cried Rick.

Another scream and another customer came up to the stage to get their certificate. I drew the third number.

"Our third and last prize, a champagne dinner for two valued at $500 here at Escalata, goes to … table number 125!" cried Justin.

The couple sitting at that table didn't look impressed. However, the woman got up and came to retrieve her certificate. When she read that the "champagne dinner" included a five-course meal, champagne, and wine, she was a little more enthusiastic.

"Congratulations, everyone, and Happy New Year! Your dessert service will begin in a few minutes," announced Justin.

All three of us left the stage and got out of the way of the servers, who were descending on the tables with the dessert course. Another set of servers were following around coffee and tea service, and yet another set of servers were following them with a liqueur trolley.

Dancing continued until 1:30, when the band stopped playing. Rick turned on the house music, but that would only be another thirty minutes, as the restaurant had to start kicking people out at 2:00.

It had been a very long day. Most of the staff in the kitchen had been there since 6:00 a.m., preparing the baked goods, bread, and entrees. When the last customer left at 2:03 a.m., Rick closed and locked the doors, and Justin called all the staff into the dining room.

Everyone took a well-deserved seat. Justin stood up with a champagne flute in his hand. "My dear staff, I don't know how to thank you. You all worked so hard today and it was an unmitigated success!" They all cheered. "Both Rick and I are so happy to let you know that there will be a $1,000 bonus for each and every one of you tomorrow. We killed it!" screamed Justin.

"He's right, I had a quick look at the take tonight, and we broke $115,000 tonight!" yelled Rick. Cheers broke out again. "That's all because of you. So thank you!"

"Tomorrow we are closed, but I personally would like to invite every one of you for dinner, cooked by Rick and I, for you. Free of charge. Yes, you may bring a plus one," announced Justin.

There were lots of murmurs and cheers now.

"Please leave your name with Rick if you will be coming, so I know how much food to make! It will be a Southern barbeque," said Justin.

"Right now, we'll let the janitors take over the cleaning. I know the kitchen is in top shape already. Don't worry about restocking until the second, when we're back in," said Rick. "Good night, everyone, and Happy New Year!"

Everyone clapped and stood up and exited out the back of the restaurant. Some pulled trash with them as they went and tossed it into the dumpsters. They were great staff.

"Have you eaten?" I asked Justin.

"Oh yeah, a chef's prerogative. I'm eating all day long!" he answered. "Don't worry about me, sunshine. By the way, I cannot say thank you enough to the immense job you did tonight for us. It really made such an amazing impression on all of our guests. If you ever want a job, girl, you're hired at triple the pay!"

"I'll keep it in mind," I said, grinning.

"Come on, let me take you home," said Rick. He grasped my hand and tucked it inside his arm. "You don't need us anymore tonight, right?" he asked Justin leadingly.

"Nope, you two lovebirds go and do your thing," he answered. "I'm going to bask in the receipts and do the books. It's my happy place after a night like tonight."

"Good night!" I said as I went with Rick. Justin had stopped listening, already closing the register and running reports.

Chapter 6

— Falon

Life has been beautiful—dare I say perfect even? thought Falon. *I probably shouldn't jinx it by saying that.*

Mark had been setting up an office here in Montreal and gradually moving some of his operations. He'd also been gradually bringing clothes and personal stuff into my apartment.

I glanced over at Mark while he was sleeping. I often lay here and recalled that day when he took the steps to start turning me into an immortal. It was a magical day, and profoundly emotional. He literally poured himself into me and gave me everything he was.

Some days I was still a bit stiff. But it all went away pretty quickly. I wasn't sure what was supposed to happen; Mark was in the dark about that too. He was born Immortal, and I was his first human transmogrification.

Deciding to get up, I walked into the bathroom and looked at myself in the mirror. I did this every day. *Do I see anything different?* Mark never left a mark on my neck from biting, but you'd think there would be something different about me after so many times.

The weirdest thing was my jaws aching. They felt a little warm, and there was a slight swelling in my jaws.

One day, I picked up the toothpaste to brush my teeth and wasn't paying attention. I squeezed and the tube exploded because I hadn't taken the cap off. Toothpaste all over the walls! *Sigh*. I was getting stronger.

The next lamebrain thing I did was when I was pouring glasses of orange juice for Mark and me. I sneezed while holding a glass and I crushed the glass. My reflex sent shards of glass flying across the kitchen. I watched in horror as the wounds in my hand closed around shards of glass.

Then the most remarkable thing happened: the glass pushed out of my hand and fell to the floor. They left no marks at all, and my hand was soon good as new.

"Are you okay, hon?" called Mark from the bathroom.

"Oh yeah, just crushed a glass is all," I called back.

He came running into the kitchen. "Did your hand heal all right?" he asked.

"Right as rain," I said. "In fact, my body pushed the glass pieces out of my hand after it healed."

"Good, I think that means you're progressing well. Our bodies don't tolerate any foreign objects. Needles, shrapnel, whatever, will be pushed out of the body."

"Bullets?"

"Yup, those too will be expelled."

"Handy," I said. "What about piercings or tattoos?"

"Nope, they too get pushed out and healed."

"What about drugs?"

"Our bodies process drugs faster, so they don't affect us as much."

That night, I decided to do an inventory check on my wounds and flaws. It had been about a week since my vision was getting blurry. I thought my vision was supposed to get better, but I couldn't see through my glasses very well anymore. Not only that, I was getting headaches from wearing them.

Starting the shower, I stripped out of my clothes and inspected myself. The small flaws and scars on my skin were fading quickly. The large scar on my leg was all but gone, and the depression in my leg where my old skating injury was had vanished. That injury happened when I was just eleven and a fellow skater and I collided in mid-air while doing jumps. I ended up on the bottom when we both fell, and her skate blade ended up cutting my leg open rather severely. In fact, a piece of muscle tissue was gone and that had left a depression in my leg. They gave me forty-eight stitches to sew me back together again.

It was like the damaged muscle in my leg had been regrown. The other small scars I'd collected over the years were gone completely as well.

I wiped the steam off the bathroom mirror with my hand and looked at my face. I could actually see my face in real detail. I picked up my glasses and put them on and instantly my head pounded and everything got blurry. I took them off and it was perfect.

Thank you, immortality! I could see perfectly now. For a woman who had worn glasses since she was six, that was a miracle. No more glasses, no more contacts, no laser surgery to think about. Nada.

I looked at the rest of myself in the mirror. I didn't usually do that. I don't like what I see usually. Does anyone? I saw I was still stuck with the same body shape. *Sigh. I guess we can't get everything! Too bad immortality doesn't fix a big ass!*

I realized the steam was pouring out of the shower. Best not to waste it. Stepping in was like being wrapped in a warm blanket.

I stood under the streaming water, letting it sluice over my head and down my breasts. It felt like Mark caressing me. So I took my breasts in hand and gently massaged them until the nipples started getting hard. They were sensitive from all the lovemaking we did last night.

Touching myself between my legs, I started a slow circular motion that had me moving my hips and my breath catching. I was hungry for Mark now. Only he could satisfy me, but the sensations touching myself were delightful.

"If I keep this up, I'll never get clean," I told myself.

"If you keep what up?" I heard from the other room.

"You're awake!"

"I'm up if that's what you mean," he chortled.

Mark walked into the shower behind me with a glorious erection leading the way.

"I heard you needed satisfaction," he murmured into my ear.

"How did you know?"

"I can smell your arousal." Mark bit me on the neck again, gently this time, with only a little fang. "My fangs aren't fully extended yet," he explained.

The sensation was delicious—a little bit of pain followed by shivers of delight. It made me rub myself harder in response and I could feel the heat rising again.

I turned toward him and looked in his eyes. I could see the arousal there too, in the swirling gold.

"Ah, your eyes are changing," he said as he nibbled my ear.

"Yes, I can see perfectly without my glasses now. I'm so happy."

"No, that's not what I mean.

"He turned me around and brought his shaving mirror to my face. I could see flecks of purple in my eyes.

"Will my eyes glow like yours?" I asked.

"Yes, apparently they'll be purple," he said. "I like purple."

Mark took one of my breasts in his hand and ran his finger around the nipple in circles, letting it get erect and hard. He turned me around to face him again and his cock pushed into me without any hesitation as he ravaged my mouth in a passionate kiss. I stood there, back up against the wall of the shower, impaled by his shaft, his mouth on mine and his hands massaging my breasts. I felt my feet leave the floor and I wrapped my legs around his hips to support myself. He raised his knee up under my ass to provide a little support as he slowly withdrew and pushed in again, reaching into me a little farther with every thrust.

He stopped kissing me because he was starting to moan so much and lose control. I held on as his pumping got harder and deeper. There was nothing I could do to help in this position—it was all Mark. His hands left my breasts, took my ass and lifted me up so he could pound in harder. He brought me down on his shaft so that he tipped me again and I could feel his head kissing the entrance to my womb. The next thing I felt was an explosion; his seed poured into me, his shaft quivering inside, my vagina squeezing him tight in response. My orgasm came a moment later as I hit the heights. He again gave me venom to launch me even higher.

My knees were weak and so were his as we slid slowly to the floor together. Still connected, with me sitting on his lap facing him, I wrapped my legs around his hips and held on to him. He embraced me and pulled my head to his chest, where I could feel his heart pounding in rhythm with mine. We sat there with the hot water running over us for quite a while.

Contentment, love, safety, all these things suffused me sitting in his embrace. God, I loved this man with all my being. I couldn't be without him. Ever.

"Falon?"

"Mmmmm?"

"I think the water is turning cold."

"Mmmmm."

"Shall we get out?"

"Mmmmm. In a minute."

"Falon?"

I wasn't answering because I wasn't really there. I was floating in my happy place, feeling one hundred percent contentment.

Mark managed to stand up with me in his arms and not dislodge himself from inside me too much—although his cock slipped a bit, not fully hard anymore. *Oh! Spoke too soon. There he goes again.* As Mark pushed himself back in, his cock expanded to fill the space. I swear it had a mind of its own.

Since I was holding on to Mark with my legs and arms, he let go of me to grab one of the big bath towels and wrap it around the both of us. He carried me over to the bed again and sat down. He then lifted up my face to kiss me tenderly.

"Good morning, beautiful lady."

"What a wonderful way to have a shower," I said.

"I cannot resist you when you smell aroused, woman. It's impossible. I have to have you. I have to be inside you when you smell like that."

"I'm not complaining. You can come and take me whenever you want. I am yours. You are mine. I belong to you, body and soul."

Mark kissed me deeply this time.

"I will take you up on that. Whenever I want? We may never get out of bed again," he jested.

"Can we pay the rent without working?" I asked practically.

"Yes, we can live off my profits for years," he answered.

"Well, then, let's never leave here. Make love to me all the time. I will not tire of it. Just think, we can go through the entire *Kama Sutra*."

His cock got even happier, extending inside me and dancing around. Mark's eyes hooded with desire, and his fangs elongated, showing me that my suggestion excited him very much.

Stretching me out on the bed on my back, he lifted my legs on either side of his hips. I raised my knees up high, giving him access to my clit while his happy self was busy dancing inside me. I squeezed my sheath to hold him, and his response was to kiss my cervix.

One of his fingers reached out and gently pried open the folds of my clit, starting a slow-motion circle that sent shivers outward through my body. Another finger joined in and rubbed the G-spot inside my vagina—the spot that went off when I had his fully expanded cock pounding into me. My breath started getting faster until I was panting, my hips jerking in response to the fingers working my body. All the while inside me, his shaft was waiting, expanding, wiggling a little, but just holding.

Just when I thought I was about to climax, Mark pulled out almost all the way and shot back inside. Pushing himself to the very end of his cock, his head pushed into my cervix and over the precipice of pleasure. Every time we made love, Mark hit all five erogenous zones inside me.

"Ah! Oh my. *Oh my*. OH MY!" I screamed as I came with a bang and my body shuddered and writhed.

Mark spilled his seed deep inside me again while he prolonged my orgasm by rubbing his fingers on my G-spot. Wave after wave crescendoed over me, leaving me feeling like a puddle, completely blissful.

When I came back to reality, I realized I had blacked out. I had been unconscious for about twenty minutes.

"I blacked out," was my observation.

"The venom has real potency when the climax is high."

"I didn't feel a bite this time."

"You were too far gone, love," he explained. "I brought you to a climax and then gave you venom, which took you out even further."

"But how did you give me venom this time?"

"A bite on the neck."

"Oh! I didn't feel it at all."

As my senses came back to me, I glanced at the clock on the wall. It was nearly 3:00 p.m. and we were still in bed! I was starving, and my stomach let out a huge growl. "Oh, someone is hungry," responded Mark. "Let me grab a cloth for us."

He sat up and rolled us both over so that I was on the bottom. Then he gently pulled himself out.

"Lift your hips so you don't leak too much. I filled you up with a lot of semen."

"I know, three times without stopping. Oh my, I don't have a bone left."

Chuckling came drifting out of the bathroom, along with sounds of him getting towels and running the water. A few moments later, he returned with another towel, some warm washcloths, and body wash.

The luxury of having someone clean you so gently is erotic, and something I invite everyone to experience at least once in their lives. It was sensual enough to get me going again, and that of course got Mark going again, because he could smell my arousal.

"Nope, not again," he said, playfully spanking my ass.

"Oh, that didn't help," I groaned. "Is this what life will be like? Sex all the time and not getting anything done?"

"You liked that?" He spanked the other cheek. Not hard, but enough to be scintillating. "If you want life to be that way, we can make it that way."

"Oh," I groaned again. "Don't do that, or I'll be grabbing him and abusing him again."

"Well, now I want to see where this goes," said Mark.

"No! I'm starving! Let's reserve this for later. We can try some things?" I asked.

"Hmmm," he said. "What kind of things?"

"Food first," I demanded with a growl.

Laughing, he finished up his ministrations and helped me to my feet. I grabbed a towel and tucked it between my legs, because I was still draining his seed from inside me.

"Wow, do you have anything left in there?" I asked as I gently grasped his balls.

He smiled wickedly. "Oh, don't worry, love. I'll make some more just for you."

Sitting at the kitchen table watching Mark cooking was a lovely treat. He was a pretty good cook, competent with the tools of the trade and creative enough to take what was there and make something up. As I watched, I realized that Mark and I needed to sit down and talk about the future—I mean really talk. It wasn't about fun anymore. We had a life-long—emphasis on long—commitment to each other. What did we do with that? *Will life be that much different? Should it be different?* When you have an unlimited amount of time to live, what do you do? The thought of just accumulating wealth seemed hollow to me.

"Hey, Mark, what now? You've turned me. What now? Do I go back to my life? Do we start a different life? Are there things I can and cannot do? Am I supposed to live in some specific way? Do I join you and Gwen?"

"Whoa, whoa, whoa!" exclaimed Mark. "First off, there is no 'supposed to.' We can choose our own lives."

"But your father—" I started.

"Wouldn't let me have a relationship with you," interrupted Mark. "That was why I was sent away. Not for any other reason."

"So you didn't have to take up a position at the family business?" I asked.

"Well, I did, but that choice was put upon me so I could learn," he answered. "Interning in a business related to your chosen field is always a good option, whether you're immortal or not."

"Yes. I agree. "So what did you intern in?"

"In the hospitality business. It's where I started with Gwen. From there, we purchased our first hotel."

"But now you do all kinds of things," I said.

"Yes, we have diversified," said Mark. "Gwen is the business head—she understands mergers and acquisitions like no other. She also has about forty years on me in terms of experience. So she is the one that decides what we invest in. The investments—buying properties—are how we earn our livelihoods. It all goes into a shared bank that the family draws from."

"So what about us?" I asked.

"We can do what we want," Mark answered. "What do you want to do?"

"I like my career, like what I get to do—I don't like the people sometimes," I said remembering the last project I was on.

"Well, there is no reason why you can't keep going. The limits for us are when our unchanging appearances start raising suspicions. That's when we have to move on. Hence the ownership of properties. Those monies go into the bank regardless of where we are or who we are."

"Every time you change identities, you have to re-establish yourself?"

"Yes, to some extent." Mark brought over the omelets he was preparing and placed two plates on the table. "Here, let's eat and then we can talk some more."

"This looks delicious!" I said, eyeing the wonderful cheese and mushroom omelet with bacon, sitting before me. He'd also warmed up some blueberry scones to go with it. Tasting a morsel, I smiled at him. "This IS delicious!" I was hungry after this morning's lovemaking; the food was filling a huge hole in my gut.

"Good, I'm glad you like it. You need to eat. The change demands a lot of your body. You need to feed it to make sure you don't get weak."

"Like what?" I asked.

"Well, for one, I imagine that being immortal means your body becomes stronger. The bones will become denser, muscles stronger, heart larger, lungs larger too. In fact, you may find that your clothes stop fitting you."

"Really?"

"Yeah, you may grow a little here and there. And health issues you may have had will be repaired or eliminated. Basically, your body will be remade into the best version of you that it can be."

"Wow."

"You need to have that in order to be able to live longer. Remember, it's not forever, just considerably longer than regular humans," he explained.

"So how much longer?"

"Our average lifespan is maybe ten times that of a human. Actually, I don't know exactly, I'm guessing. No one in my family talks about that. I don't know how only my parents are. They won't say. It will be long enough to see big changes in society—and to effect big changes too."

"What sort of big changes have you made?" I asked.

"Well, one of my pet projects is to provide education to those who don't usually have access to it. We try to get schools built in remote areas. It's hard because we run into politics everywhere we go."

"How do you pay for that?"

"Through our bank," he answered. "There are ample funds in there to achieve whatever we can think of."

"Which bank is it?"

"It's a family-run bank. We own it, operate it, and it's passed down through the centuries to each generation. The specific family that runs it—cousins of mine—holds the title to the bank in perpetuity. Their ancestors and their descendants operate the bank on behalf of the family. It is not connected to any other financial institution—so it's the most secure bank on the planet. Not even Switzerland can claim that title," he explained.

"So let's get back to what you want to do," Mark said as he got up and cleared the dishes.

I picked up my coffee, walked into the living room, and sat on the couch. "That was yummy, Mark. Thanks for making brunch."

Gazing out the patio doors, winter life was all around us. People were walking dogs, cross-country skiing, waiting for buses, or driving somewhere in their cars. Life was happening.

Not too long ago that was me, and I hadn't had a second thought about it. It was just life. I went to the market on

Sundays. I did my laundry on Saturdays. I went to work on Monday. When my last project finished, I took time off and Mark and I spent a few weeks in Houston. And now? Workwise, I didn't know what was next.

Mark came and joined me on the couch. Drawing me into his arms, he pulled me up against his body. I leaned back against his chest. It felt safe here inside the circle of his arms. I never wanted to leave. I realized I was addicted to his presence. The thought of him going brought me to tears—which was so completely full of shit. Still, snuggling was nice, so I indulged myself.

"What do you want to do now?" he asked me again.

"I like my job, and I like working for Peter and Norman. Their projects are interesting…"

"Okay, then continue like nothing has changed for you. After all, as far as they're concerned, nothing has changed. You're still Falon Robertson, and still are the same beautiful woman they sent to Georgia."

"What will you do?" I asked.

"I will keep going on what I do too," he replied. "With one major exception: I will finish moving my base of operations to Montreal.

"Will that be safe? You look different, so you won't be recognized by anyone?"

"Correct. Only my family will know me."

"So no big changes other than that for now?" I asked.

"Nope. No need. You can come back down to Houston too."

Chapter 7

— Lora

My kids were scheduled to be with me for the March break week, but their father wanted to take them. He'd decided to take them on another ski trip to Mont Tremblant because they all had so much fun. I suspected he was trying to be "the good guy" and buy them with gifts. It'd work, cause my kids were typical, cynical teens.

But that meant I would be on my own, which didn't happen very often. Rick and I spoke on the phone every day, but it wasn't enough. Opportunities to spend time together were rare, which was why I hated "long-distance romances." But this one was different, we were really bonded somehow. So, I wanted to make the most of this gift of a week off.

My thoughts were always occupied with Rick and the opportunity to spend more time with him. We'd last spent time together at New Year's when I went down for a whole week. It was glorious.

This time, with my kids being away, perhaps he could come to Montreal for a change. We had talked about my kids and how important they were to me. He agreed with my reasoning. We weren't going to disrupt their lives until we knew we were more than just a mutual craving.

But it wasn't just sex. We shared a deep connection I'd never felt before.

Falon believed Rick and I had wild sex that first weekend we spent together. She was right. We did. The sex was going to happen from the moment we laid eyes on each other. But that wasn't all there was. The truth of it was that even then we connected. I mean, we really connected about all kinds of things. Big cosmic things and small things. We talked about emotions—yes, emotions—with a guy! I told him I was a witch and he didn't even flinch. Now, maybe he didn't believe me, or maybe he just thought I meant something else, but he didn't make any snide comments.

Then we had Hallowe'en together. That was magical. I think that was the first time I truly relaxed around a man. He treated me like a queen, and I felt so comfortable with him. Comfortable enough that I didn't feel the urge to "entertain him" or keep the conversation going, or even that I had to be dressed. I was comfortable enough to wear my worst PJs and go around without makeup and just sit and read quietly.

I *didn't* walk around in PJs or without makeup—that would be a deadly sin! But I felt it wouldn't matter if I *did*.

My holiday at New Year's, well, that was transformative. We'd talked seriously about the future. I was actually considering that there was a future. That's not something I'd ever had. My kids' father was not someone I had seen a future with.

I intended on getting down and dirty with Rick for that week. I wanted to explore our sexual connection as much as we explored each other's minds. Since meeting Rick, I'd not been interested in any other men. I kept dreaming of my nights with him. I didn't want anyone else.

What's more, the sex was amazing! Like Falon-type amazing. Falon told me about how good Mark and her were together. Before I met Rick, I was definitely a little jealous. I couldn't even believe sex could be that good. It was always wham-bam-thank you, ma'am.

Rick? He always satisfied me first! *Me first!* And when we connected, oh my Goddess, talk about a perfect fit. No guy had ever reached that far inside me before! *Oh, Goddess, you have given me a great gift. I know I'm repeating myself, but thank you.* I couldn't believe he reached all five erogenous zones inside me. I'd had lots of partners, but bar none, Rick fit me like a glove.

For the first time since my last child was born, I wanted to be with someone. I wanted to get to know them. I believe he felt the same way.

I was daydreaming about our lovemaking, and becoming aroused at the sensation of him deep inside me, when the phone rang.

"Lora?" came that sultry Southern voice. "It's Rick. Did I catch you at a bad time?"

"Rick, um no, I was just thinking about New Year's," I said, clearing my throat. "Not a bad time, no." I grinned.

"Are you alone?"

"Yup, just me here. My kiddlings are off with their father today."

"I wish I was there with you," he said, laden with emotion.

"That's exactly what I was hoping you'd say," said Lora. "It just so happens that my kids will be away for a whole week this month—for March break—in two weeks. So … I was hoping that perhaps we could find a way of spending time together. It's a big ask with the distance, but I thought I'd put it out there and see."

"That's probably quite do-able," he answered. "Do you want to come here, or shall I come to Montreal?"

"Well, it's cold here right now. March in Montreal is lots of fun, but it can snow as easily as it gets hot," I said. "So what do you think?"

"I wouldn't mind coming to you. After all, you came here last time, so it's my turn to travel."

"If you're interested, we can do St. Patrick's Day. It's a Friday this year."

"I tell you what, let me make sure Justin doesn't have anything special planned for St. Patrick's here and get back to you later today?"

"That's better than I had expected!" I said excitedly. "Looking forward to hearing from you again. In the meantime, I'll see what I can organize on my end."

"Bye, Lora," he said.

Nothing ventured, nothing gained, I say. This could be wonderful. I'd have to let Falon and Mark know, because maybe they'd want to join us one day.

Chapter 8

— Rick

When I got off the phone, I felt blown away.

After the week Lora had spent at New Year's, I'd fallen firmly and irrevocably in love with her. I hadn't expected to ever love this hard again. It was difficult because she lived so far away. Only hearing from that delectable woman occasionally made me yearn all the more for her.

She had really rocked my world—even more than Falon had. The two of them were very similar—but very different too. Initially, I was attracted to Falon, but once I saw my green-eyed bombshell, Falon was a distant memory, especially since she was with Mark.

Since my wife's death, I'd dated a few times, but most women just didn't challenge my mind enough, and that was what I was drawn to most. Physical appearance was all fine and well, but if they didn't have it going on upstairs, then I'm just not interested for long.

Lora was a bonus package, a gorgeous petite Irish woman with fiery emerald-green eyes and luscious black hair down to her ass. Her curves were mature, and her bones were padded just perfectly. I am tall at 6 ft 3, so I liked the fact that Lora fit under my arm nicely. I loved that she wasn't obsessed with her weight, and she loved to eat. I was so tired of skinny women who wouldn't eat anything in fear of gaining a pound.

Putting the phone down, I left my office and went looking for Justin. It was he who planned the menu. I, being a pastry chef, was responsible for offering a selection of complementary sweets to go with the entrees Justin put together.

Our restaurant was doing so well that we could afford to hire chefs to do most of the cooking, but one of the partners had to be on hand every day to make sure the chefs and sous-chefs kept standards up. Since winning the James Beard award last year, our patronage had doubled to the point that we hired a full-time manager to take care of staff and premises, as well as the books. It left Justin and I time to create.

We were hoping to get another award this year. Certainly, we were working hard enough to deserve it. It was more difficult to get an award in your second and subsequent years in business than your first year. When you're new and shiny, you get lots of attention.

"Hey, Justin, are you planning anything special for St. Patrick's Day this year?" I asked when I found him.

"Ah, no. Did you want to?" Justin replied, a bit puzzled. He got nervous. "We don't usually—at least we didn't last year. Do you think we need to start doing holidays too?"

"Calm down, this question doesn't mean I was thinking of that. I just got an invitation from Lora to visit her in a couple of weeks. It spans over St. Patrick's Day. I didn't want to leave you with an event if you had one planned."

"Oh! Well, that's different," he said. "Of course you'll go to Montreal. And while you're there, get to some restaurants and see if you can find some ideas!"

"I will try. I tell you what, I'll make sure the week is planned for so that there will be a good variety of desserts, and give Juan the shopping list for the week. I'll make sure the sous-chefs can manage the offerings."

"That's cool. We can handle it," agreed Justin.

I walked back down to the office and called Lora back.

"Hey there," she answered.

"It's a go!" I said excitedly. "I've arranged with Justin to have the menu planned in advance, and there is nothing special we're doing for that day, so he won't need me on hand."

"Excellent! Let me know what your flight will be, and I can pick you up if you like. The kids *should be* gone by Sunday at 5:00. But, their father is always late, so I would not plan on being here before 9:00 p.m. if you want to avoid meeting him."

"Got it. I'll get a flight that lands in the evening. If I have to, I can find my own way there and waste time at the airport. I don't want to miss a single minute with you."

"Aww, that's so sweet. I've got to warn you though—my place is not fancy. It's a simple townhouse with four tiny bedrooms. I live in an older part of the city. I don't have a big house, or servants, or a fancy back yard—and I'm not the best of housekeepers," she admitted.

"Don't worry, mamacita, I'm there for you, not your house," I said "What kind of clothes will I need?"

"Well, that's the $64,000 question. We could get weather that delivers early summer temperatures, mid-winter temperatures, or both. So I'll let you know closer to the day you travel."

"I can always go shopping there if I need something."

"Yup. And if the clothes don't work in Atlanta, you can always keep them here for the next time," she blurted out.

"Do I get my own closet now?"

"I will make room in my closet for your Montreal clothes, how about that?" she asked.

"You mean my pants will be rubbing up against your dresses?" I asked suggestively. A moment later, I could swear I *heard* her smirk over the phone. How do you hear a smile?

"I guess they will be," she said. "What you goin' to do 'bout it? Eh?"

Laughing out loud now, I said "Does that make them happy pants?"

"This is getting silly," Lora said. "So let me know what the specifics are, please."

"I will. See you soon."

I hung up the phone and was whistling a happy tune as I went about the rest of my day. March was going to be a good month.

Chapter 9

— Lora

Falon called me a few days later to catch up. That gave me the opportunity to let her know that Rick was coming up to Montreal for March break week. When she heard the news, she squealed in delight.

"Oh, that's great news, Lora!"

"Yes, it is going to be nice to have him here. I'll get to see him in a setting that isn't luxurious. I wonder how he likes doing dishes?"

"You're not going to make him do dishes, girl!"

"No, I'm not. I expect we'll be spending little time outside of the bedroom."

"So it's going that well?"

"Let's just say, Rick is my Mark. I cannot believe the connection I have to him, but frankly I'm not going to waste time denying it either. I think there is really something there. But I need to be sure—as much as anything I can be sure of—before I commit to this guy. After all, we have the same problem you and Mark had with distance. I can't assume he'll want to move here too."

"But you can dream," said Falon. "So are we going to double date while he's here, or are you going to keep him all to yourself?"

"I was thinking of a pub crawl on Friday—you know like we did last year when Mark came to Montreal for the first time? Rick hasn't experienced our 'pub crawl' yet."

"That sounds like fun, I'll get Mark's take on it."

"Well, why don't you come over and we can plan St. Patty's Day together?"

"Will do. It's been a couple of months since we had a girls' night. I'll be there in … say, forty-five minutes?"

"Sounds good."

Life had been busy, so this was a great opportunity to do some girl time.

When the doorbell rang and Falon came in, I immediately sensed something different about her.

"Falon, what has changed in you?" I looked her straight in the eye. One of her eyebrows lifted at the query.

"Um, nothing much," she said. I think she hoped I wouldn't push it.

"Na ah, ah," I shook my finger. "That doesn't work on me. Spill it. I sense something different."

"I am turning," she said quietly. "But you can't reveal that to anyone. I mean it! Look at this."

She opened her mouth to show me her canine teeth had sharpened and elongated a little.

"I knew it! I knew something was different! You're becoming one of them!" I cried. "I'm aware of the need for secrecy. It's safe with me. When did this start?"

"How did you know? Uh, back in August, we had unprotected sex. Yeah, that was stupid, but I wasn't really thinking that night. Oh God, it was so hot."

"I'm not sure, I just sensed something was different about you," I answered. "I was picking up some sort of energy. Back to how: so you had unprotected sex. The worst that usually happens is STDs. What was different?"

"He bit me."

"Hmmm, yeah, that's happened before. We know he's like Zisis. Oh ... oh!"

"Yes. I got a double dose with his semen and his venom. Now I'm experiencing a few new things—like this," she said, pulling out a small knife from her bag. She cut a small wound into her hand and then wiped away the blood.

"No! That is not what I meant. Rick told me he had the overwhelming urge to bite me!" I said as I watched as the blood welled up and ran off her hand. Then the two edges of the cut just went back together like nothing happened.

"Oh. My. Goddess," I said.

"That's not the only thing that has changed. My eyesight has improved. I don't need glasses anymore. So I'll have to tell people I'm wearing my lenses all the time or that I had laser surgery. My hearing is also better."

"I think laser surgery is better," I said. "Wait, did you say *venom*?"

"Yes, I said venom," she said. "Okay, I've told you about Zisis and Mark. They were the same person. They're immortals. Immortals have fangs, like movie vampires, but they don't drink blood with them. They're actually defensive weapons and deliver venom. When we have sex—oh-my-God-Lora-the-best-sex-ever!—when he hits his climax, he is compelled to bite me and this delivers venom. But during lovemaking the venom takes on a different property. It's an aphrodisiac and enhances the female's orgasm. It's like nothing you have ever had with a human."

"Some of this you've said before—what's different?" I asked

"Unprotected sex and consent. He asked me if he could bite me and I said yes. He basically emptied himself—I mean emptied. He was drained and for the first time, limp afterward."

"He doesn't go limp after orgasm?" I asked.

"Not normally," said Falon. "He can go five rounds and not be—you know—finished."

"Geez, Falon, that's exactly like Rick," I said. "Do you think…?"

"What do you mean?" asked Falon. "Whoa, you said just a second ago he has the urge to bite you too?"

"The last time we were together, at New Year's, we had a particularly raunchy lovemaking session. After he was spent, he told me he had the incredible urge to bite me. We didn't get into it. Now I wish I had. I'll have to ask him when he comes to Montreal."

"Lora, is Rick like Mark?"

"I don't know! Maybe?" I said. "What else is happening to you?"

"My body has been repairing itself. All the injuries I have had are being repaired like I never had them. Scars I had have disappeared too. Remember the scar on my arm from the rabbit bite?"

"Yeah."

"Look!" Falon rolled up her sleeve and showed me where there had been a small, squarish scar from a rabbit biting her. It was gone and the skin looked completely unblemished.

"Wow, that is remarkable," I said. "Anything else?"

"I'm getting stronger and faster. I may not be as strong or as fast as Mark, but I'll be better than a human. He's been teaching me how to do things like shadow walk."

"I've heard of that. Let's see," I encouraged her.

"Okay, I'll shadow walk to the kitchen and grab a cup and come back," she said. In one second, she blinked out of existence and was back handing me a cup.

"That's a cool trick!"

"I know, eh!" she cried. "Oh! And our hearts are synchronized. I can feel his heart beating like mine. It's like I'm never alone."

"Aw, that's magical," I said. "I'm a little jealous. This is a very special honor very few humans will ever hear of, much less experience. Be careful with these powers, Falon. You're in my world now, and it's not always rainbows and sunshine."

We caught up on the rest of the stuff and got to planning our activities for when Rick arrived. Falon wasn't assigned any special job right now, so she wasn't going to be traveling.

"I'm liking the idea of doing St. Patrick's Day again this year," she said. "It was a good idea when you suggested it. It was a very special weekend and when Mark and I fucked our brains out the first time!"

"I remember. I was solo, so it was okay—fun, but it's difficult being a third wheel. At least I got a hook-up that night. We could plan a double date this year, and this time I'll have my own special guy with me."

"That would be so cool. We could do the carriage ride together and throw innuendo back and forth. Mark and Rick got along really well in Miami."

"Oh, remember their faces when we got off the elevator dressed up?"

"Oh ya! I thought they'd be drooling all night long," she chuckled.

"We need to go shopping!"

"Definitely," agreed Falon.

"Okay, so Friday we'll do a double date. Should we book a suite so we can have a little ritzy hanky-panky?"

"Hmm, the Ritz Carlton would be a nice place to spend the night. I'm sure they have suites with hot tubs," she said. "But if we're going swanky, we can't just go bar hopping. We'd be overdressed—unless you had a special place in mind?"

"No, you're right. Friday would need to be casual. But we should still have a hotel suite booked in case we're too drunk to drive. So what do we do on Saturday?"

"Let's find out what's in town. Perhaps there's a good concert, or a cool show?" suggested Falon.

"Maybe we should just keep it casual. We could do some fun things like a jazz club, or live music, or visit Old Montreal, or what about the biodome?"

"Hmmm, good ideas. Maybe we let the guys decide. Where should we start though?" asked Falon.

I had received an email from Rick letting me know his flight schedule. He was arriving at 9:30 p.m. tonight. That was perfect. The kids should be picked up by then, and I'd have some time to clean the house a bit. I'm not a good housekeeper, but I wanted the place to look good.

Picking up the toys and clothes from the kids, I basically distributed that back to their rooms and closed their doors. I vacuumed and picked up my living room and made the bathrooms and kitchen spotless. I paid particular attention to my bedroom, putting new bedding on it, getting out my crystals, and setting some candles ready for lighting.

I heard a car pull up; checking my watch, it was 6:45. The kids were screaming and yelling in excitement because their father had arrived. He was late as usual, but not so late that it caused a problem this time.

"Lora, I'm bringing them back next Sunday?" he yelled through the front door.

"Yes please," I yelled back. I heard the door close and the car take off. Taking a deep, cleansing breath, I relaxed several notches. Now it was just about me and Rick.

My bedroom was ready, the house picked up. I drew myself a bath and had a good soak. I waxed everything to give myself a silky-smooth complexion everywhere, applied lotion all over to make my skin soft and scented nicely, and took off the old nail polish and washed my long hair. *That will take an hour to dry by itself. I'll put it up in a braid so that it stays neat, and waves when I take it out.*

I picked out some loose but clingy, wide-leg pants and a shirt to match. No buttons, zippers, or ties to undo. Pull on, pull off. Neither did I put on a bra, but I did put on a thong. It had a butterfly in the front. It was basically transparent fabric except for the butterfly.

He'll love it.

I reached for my Goddess Oil and saw that there was almost none left. Goddess Oil was a perfume I made magically, derived from some magical plants that I blended together and extracted their oils. It was an aphrodisiac when ingested, as in licked. Not that I needed any help in that area, but it contained some pheromones to heighten responses. Plus it just plain smelled amazing.

I went downstairs to my kitchen and started the process of making some more. It would take a few days to complete, but I must never run out of Goddess Oil. It was essential, and I applied a tiny bit in all the best places. Checking the time, it was 9:05. *He'll be landing soon!* I decided to use minimal makeup just to enhance my eyes and lips, two of my best features.

Feeling sexy, pretty, and confident, I sat for a few minutes and meditated to calm my soul. I was too excited. I wanted to be in the moment and not miss anything.

My phone rang, and I broke my meditation to go get it.

"Hello there," said Rick.

"Hi, are you here safe and sound?" I answered.

"I'm just outside your door," he said. "The plane was a little early, so I thought I would get a cab and see if there were kids here."

"How did you determine there weren't any?" I asked.

"The footprints in the snow showing them getting into a car."

"How very efficient of you!" I said. "Come on in, the door is unlocked."

Hanging up, I ran downstairs and waited on the bottom step. My heart was racing again. When he walked in the door, it felt like all the cylinders in a giant lock tumbled into place and my world opened up. I gasped at the sensation shooting through me. It almost felt like an orgasm, but it didn't have that same urgent feeling. It was gentle but complete.

He was beautiful. His hair was slicked back but a little bit was dangling over his forehead. He was wearing a big puffy coat and carrying one suitcase. No boots, no gloves, coat open, and underneath I could see his shirt was mostly undone.

Rick stood there frozen for a moment staring at me, his jaw agape, until he realized he was staring. I walked over to him and placed my finger on his lips.

"You're catching flies," I said.

Growling, he caught my fingertip in between his lips and sucked it inside his mouth, and gently bit down on it.

"Oh, I'm the fly?" I asked.

He dropped his bag, shrugged off his coat, and wrapped his arms around me.

"It has been too long since I've held you, Lora. I am starving for you," he murmured. "I cannot believe how good it is to see you again. You take my breath away."

"You say such wonderful things," I purred. "Come inside, let me take your bag upstairs. I have some snacks and some wine ready, unless you'd like to do something else?"

Grinning like the Cheshire Cat, Rick tightened his hold on me. "You think you're going to get away from me that easily?"

He was pressing himself into my breasts and the friction was already causing them to ripple and stand out. He glanced down at me and knew what was going through my mind. Reaching down and grabbing my ass with his cold hands, he lifted me up so that our lips were even. I wrapped my arms around his neck and he pressed his mouth against mine with a ferocity demanding entry and taking it. The sensation of his cold hands on my ass was causing me to shiver, and not with cold either. His hunger matched mine as we bruised our mouths on each other, our tongues diving and probing. I was feeling my tongue all the way around his mouth when I came across something sharp and yipped.

Pulling away slightly, I looked deeply into his eyes and didn't break contact with him. My recent conversation with Falon fresh in my mind, I watched as a pair of fangs slowly elongated in front of me and his lips opened to accommodate them.

"My, my, what have we here?" I asked. A zing of electricity pulsed through me, setting all of my nerve endings on high alert.

"When you told me you were a witch, I was so relieved that you were a member of the supernatural world. I wouldn't have to hide who I was from you," he answered.

"And who or what are you?" I asked, though I thought I knew.

"I don't know exactly. I'm not human though, that I know," he said.

"Well, this is just too erotic for me. Either you fuck me till I scream right now, or we put that on hold until we talk about this. Because I'm equally torn in two directions."

"I can wait. Just being here with you has relaxed my soul somehow. I've been so wired and coiled like a spring, waiting until I see you again."

"Maybe you're relaxed some, I'm not! Geez, the electricity is pulsing through me right now from arousal."

"I will satisfy you, woman, better than you ever have before, I promise."

I believed him.

Leading him over to the couch, I sat him down, dropped another kiss on him, and he massaged my shoulders.

"Wait here a sec," I said. I went and grabbed the wine, glasses, and tray of food I had prepped, and brought it out to the living room.

"Here, could you please open the wine for us while I take your bag upstairs? I need a moment to dispel some energy so I can hear you."

"My pleasure," he said.

Upstairs, I quickly did some breathing to draw in calm and release some of the sexual energy I was feeling. I needed to be able to control this. *I can't just jump his bones every time I see him!* Well, I could, but I shouldn't want to. Shouldn't *need* to.

While I was upstairs, I looked in the mirror and did a silent scream of delight. He was supernatural, and I thought I knew what he was. *How does he not?* Once I felt calm, I grabbed my grimoire and brought it downstairs with me and placed it on my altar table and sat beside him.

Turning toward him on the couch, I was looking into his beautiful eyes. I hadn't noticed they were a copper brown before. He handed me a glass, and as our fingers touched, sparks of electricity flew between them, zinging both of us. I felt it deep in my core, so I thought he probably did too.

A glance down showed just how much he did feel it.

"So you're supernatural," I started. "How do you not know what you are?"

"That's easy," he said. "I was adopted. My human parents adopted me when I was just a baby at eighteen months. They had no idea I wasn't human."

"When did you realize you weren't human?" I asked.

"When I was involved in a school bus crash in grade four. Nearly everyone on the bus was killed but me. Only one other kid survived. She was left a quadriplegic. I walked away with some scratches and a couple of broken bones. I don't know how. One minute the bus was driving along the road, the next minute it was flying through the air rotating around its long axis, and then plunging into a river."

"Oh my, that would have been traumatic."

"I was terrified they would blame me. But they never did. I was found under the bus where it washed up, all banged up. But that's not what gave me a clue. It was how fast I healed," he explained.

"What do you mean?" I asked.

"I was rushed to the hospital and they discovered I had broken bones. The doctors figured I would be in casts for about eight weeks. A few hours later, they returned to my bed to put the cast on my leg and noticed all the contusions were gone. They figured the chart was wrong. They told me to come back in two weeks to make sure the breaks were lined up properly. Those x-rays showed the breaks had already healed completely like it had never been there. They stood around and scratched their heads for a couple of hours, but eventually they declared that the x-ray showing that break must have belonged to someone else. They removed the casts and let me go."

"Wow! That's quite the story. What else has happened?" I asked.

"Since then, I've never been injured very long, and I'm very strong, stronger than most people my size. I joined the weightlifting team in high school, and when I started to outpace the other students in my weight class by double and triple the weight, I stopped. People were starting to talk behind my back. After that, I've hidden anything I've noticed that is not 'normal,'" he said with air quotes.

"So you got married? You said you had children," said Lora.

"Yes, I married my college sweetheart. We were madly in love, or so I thought, but she was not interested in marriage, only in having kids. It was during my marriage to her that I discovered another aspect of my non-humanness."

"What was that?"

"I grow fangs when I get really, really aroused. The first time it happened I nearly shit myself. I was with Meredith, my wife. It wasn't the first time we had made love, but that particular time, for some reason, she really got into it, and that brought me further along with her. There was a little dominance play, and she started to enjoy herself. I was behind her, and she didn't see, but I happened to be facing a mirror. My eyes were glowing, and I had fangs hanging out of my mouth. What's more … the need to bite her when I climaxed. I didn't give into that, but it was really difficult."

"Did you ever? Bite her?" I asked.

"No. Never did. Every time I resisted. But sex became mundane quickly. She became bored, I wasn't excited as much, and then she had our daughter. She was a good mother. Her heart was into having children and she begged me for another. Our son was born a year later. They had the benefit of a mama until they were nearly out of their teens. After our son was born, we never had sex again. She just wasn't interested. Then illness took her and we were all broken for a while."

"Wow, that's rare, and difficult to live with," sympathized Lora.

"It wasn't so difficult. We were close and very good friends. She was my best friend. We worked well together raising our kids too. She was the one who encouraged me to become a chef. I did all the cooking at home, and she saw my talent and made me do something with it."

"So she never saw this other you? Did anyone else?" I asked.

"You're the only other woman I've been with. Well, that's not exactly true, Falon and I almost got into it. We had started when the phone rang with an emergency. Isn't life funny that way? I had felt a pull toward her, but that all vanished the moment I saw you, like a puff of smoke. You became the only woman I wanted," he said, looking into my eyes. His eyes were not disguising the desire inside at all—it was all out there on display. It was intoxicating to be wanted so much.

Clearing my throat with a swallow, I took his hand.

"Do you want to know what you are?" I asked him.

"Yes, most definitely. But I don't scare you, do I? I don't think I could live with myself if I scared you away," he said, worried.

"No, you're not going to scare me away. I've seen many other things in my life that are way scarier! Besides, call me weird, I think it's kind of sexy—the whole intense eyes and fangs thing. It turns me on like nothing I've ever experienced before."

It was true. When I saw those fangs, my coil tightened inside as my body said *Yes! Praise Jesus!* It had notched itself halfway to a climax already. Sitting there being calm was using up my self control.

"Um, there is one other thing," he said.

"And that is…?"

"I can smell a woman's arousal. My sense of smell is rather good, and I can detect different emotions, and the strongest of those is arousal."

"So you know what's happening inside me right now, don't you?" I asked with a big smile on my face.

"Um, yes. It's also intoxicating," he admitted.

"Since we're intoxicating each other, I think we should do something about it—quickly," I suggested.

Chapter 10

— Lora

Rick and I went upstairs and made love. It was powerful, exciting, and very erotic. Knowing that we were both supernatural, it made sense why we connected so deeply. We shared that energy, and this time neither of us held back.

When he nearly brought me to my fourth orgasm, he was ready to blow himself. He hesitated and looked at me with those copper eyes swirling with power. His fangs were elongated about one and half inches and they were dripping venom. He paused for a moment while he was deep inside me. I could feel him twitching with excitement as his orgasm had nearly taken him.

"Lora, my need to bite you is overwhelming. I don't think I will be able to stop myself this time. I'm losing control of myself," he admitted. "Can you pass me a pillow and I'll bite it?"

I looked up at him and pulled his head to me and his mouth on mine. I licked his fangs, pricking my tongue a bit, and I felt him shudder as my action made him even harder inside me.

"Oh, don't do that. It'll end everything very quickly," he admitted.

So I licked him again, and pushed my tongue into his mouth. He devoured me and his cock started moving again, faster this time.

As he slammed into me, reaching my cervix, he released his seed, the force of which I could feel even through my own orgasm. I tilted my head and gave him access to my neck. Rick groaned and bent down to my shoulder. I felt a momentary prick of pain followed by the most euphoric rush I had ever had. I rocketed out of my body and was floating above us.

Rick's cock was still moving inside me as his whole body shuddered with the release. My back arched to move my hips up to meet him, and the intensity of my own orgasm left me feeling like gelatin as I lay there.

I blacked out. I know I did, because there was a period of time I just could not recall. When my mind returned, Rick was lying on top of me, nearly comatose himself. I turned my head to peer at him. One of his eyelids lifted and he peered back at me from over by my shoulder.

"Oh my, that was different," I understated. "Rick, you've been holding back on me." I grinned at my own clever tease.

"Not intentionally," he said. "I didn't know that would happen. What just happened?"

"As far as I can tell, your bite delivers some sort of aphrodisiac or a euphoric drug, which shoots me through another orgasm. I lost count how many I had. That's never happened."

"I did that? Well, I'm pleased I was able to pleasure you properly," he said with pride in his voice.

"Properly? That doesn't begin to describe it!" I exclaimed. "Wow!"

I'd had a lot of sex partners—lots. Easily dozens. I was promiscuous—well, I *was*, not anymore. If I could get sex like this from Rick, I'd never want another human again! *Human schuman!* Fuck me! I mean … *fuck* … *me.* Holy Goddess of all, that was the very best.

"Let me take care of you," said Rick. "Tip up for me."

He lifted off me so that I could tip up a bit, and then he pulled out of me slowly. He was still solid! Oh my! What a lovely penis. Beautifully shaped. A small gush of fluids dribbled down my slit as he released the dam. Rick got up and looked for the bathroom, where he found some washcloths and towels. He returned and lovingly washed my lady parts and did his best to dry them off before placing a towel under my ass. Then he washed himself. He was standing straight out as if to say, "Hey I'm here and I want to play some more."

I sat up and grasped his cock with both hands. That made him gasp and look down at what I was doing.

"He's a saucy boy, isn't he?" I asked. "He hasn't finished playing."

"He's never finished playing," said Rick. "An orgasm doesn't bring him down again. Sometimes it's embarrassing."

"Never ever be embarrassed by that!" I cried. "Goddess forbid you are ashamed of what she's given you. You're beautiful and perfect."

I was caressing his cock, and he was responding by donating some pearls of liquid. I sucked them off his tip with my lips, pressing down around his head.

Rick's knees nearly buckled as his body responded to my hands and tongue. He placed his hands on my shoulders. His eyes were glowing again, and his breath was coming faster.

I increased my movements, using my tongue to lick his length, my lips to kiss his head, and finally to envelop him with my mouth. Using a trick I had learned years ago to suspend my gag reflex, I opened my throat and took most of him into my mouth. He watched as I pushed him farther in. He sucked in breath and he started growing again.

I felt his cock dance in my mouth, the excitement building in his body.

"I'm going to come soon," he warned me.

I hummed a *yes*, which vibrated on his cock. He giggled and gasped at the same time.

"That felt different," he said.

I pulled him out of my mouth and sped up my sucking. In and out, I pushed and pulled, using my hands on his scrotum and the base of his cock to create pressure. His cock elongated and thickened just before he exploded in my mouth. I swallowed as he squirted, which was like drinking from a fountain.

"Ah, *ah*, AH, gods!" he cried with his orgasm. "Oh, Lora, let me hold you," he growled after his seed was spent and I had released him.

He picked me up and laid me back on the bed and fell beside me. He gathered me up in his arms and held on to me like I would float away.

"To think, this is just the beginning of our week together," I said. "I suspect we're going to break some records together."

"I think I'm addicted to you, Lora," said Rick. "I'm not sure I could ever leave you again. I'll just have to move up here, because I never want to be without you."

"Rick, this is only our fourth time together—well, not sex-wise, but spending time together. You can't say that yet!"

But he could, because…

"Okay, I'll admit it," I said, "I feel the same way. I never want another lover, ever. That bite, the way you fill me, the way we fit together, it's like we were made for one another. I've never been one to believe such things, but I gotta say, if there is such a thing as fated love, you're mine," I admitted. "You were made for me, Rick Benal."

"Well, let's see where we're at by the end of the week," he said.

"I have to call Falon," I said suddenly.

"Why?"

"Because Mark is like you!"

"You mean like me, as in … not human?" he asked.

"Yes!" I cried. "He's not human, and he has fangs."

"I thought I was a vampire, but I've never wanted to drink blood and I never died—well, I don't think so."

"No, you're not a vampire. They don't exist. You're a member of an immortal group of humanoids known as the Olde Ones—you call yourselves immortals. No one knows your origin, really. They were old before humans started recording history. Your species predates man."

"How come people don't know about us?"

"For the same reason you hid what you were. People are afraid of things they don't understand. I hide my witchy self from most people. They think I'm Wiccan, which I am, but they think that's just a religion."

"Being a witch is more?" he asked.

"Yes, I'm a descendant of a cross between the Olde Ones and humans. My power comes from your line. While I worship the Goddess and the God, they are my ancestors too. The Olde Ones had godlike power compared to humans. Still do," I explained.

"Wait, who are the Olde Ones?" ask Rick.

"Let me back up a bit. I have a family book that contains a very large family tree that goes back several hundred years. It traces the lineage of the witches in my family. I found it in my mother's things after she died. The first name at the top of the tree is Aedanmar. Her parents are listed as unknown 'Olde Ones.' My research into that showed that what the witches called Olde Ones were in fact a species of immortal beings who lived on this planet too, but hidden from humanity."

"So, is there an entire species like me?"

"Yes, but there's more: when an Olde One has a child with a human, that child inherits abilities, they can become witches if they are trained. As a witch, I am not immortal, I'm a mortal supernatural. You're an immortal supernatural."

I let that sink in. I could see the wheels turning in his head. There was practically steam coming out of his ears. He looked up at me after a few minutes; his eyes were clear, and there was resolve in them somehow. He sniffed the air very delicately.

"You're very excited, not sexually, but excited nonetheless," he observed. "Do you really think I am one of these Olde Ones?"

"Yes. Falon and I have been comparing notes for the past year. I discovered Mark was an Olde One on my own, before she told me. Mark has since turned her. That happened last August, I'm sure of it, because she was just telling me all the new changes she's undergoing."

"Let's do that, then. I'm game," said Rick enthusiastically.

"Let's do what?" I asked.

"Let's turn you too."

"Wow, I never even thought about that. I've got to think about that one, Rick."

"Whatever you want to do is perfect with me," he said. "No pressure. Now, what are we doing this week?"

I didn't get a hold of Falon until a day and a half later. We solidified plans for Friday night when the four of us would meet up. Then I dropped the bomb on her.

"Falon, remember our conversation a few days ago, when I thought Rick may be like Mark?"

"Did you confirm that?"

"I did. He's got fangs!" I said excitedly.

"He has fangs like Mark has fangs?" she asked.

"Yes!"

"Wow, does that mean he's one of them too?"

"I think so," I said. Then I started to tell her Rick's story. She listened for a few minutes, then interrupted me.

"Wait, hold on to that story. Let me put you on speaker. Mark needs to hear this too," she said. I could hear her putting the phone down and calling Mark.

"What's up? asked Mark as I heard him walk into the room.

"Mark, Lora and I are having the most fascinating conversation ever, and you need to hear it. Lora, start over if you wouldn't mind, please?"

"Okay, Mark, I think Rick is a member of your species," I started.

"What!"

"Wait for it, hun, the story is amazing," said Falon. "Please proceed, Lora."

So I started over with Rick's story: his adoption, his self-discovery, all the way to the mind-blowing sex we just had and the bite. When I was finished, Mark and Falon were utterly silent on the other end. After a minute, I was afraid they had hung up on me.

"Hello? Guys? Are you still there?" I asked.

"Ya, we're here," they said together.

"So let me get this straight … Rick has glowing eyes like me, fangs like me, that come out when he's aroused, and deliver a euphoric drug on orgasm like me?" asked Mark.

"That is the case. Yes," I said.

"Wow! I don't think our family knows of any other immortals, so this is ground-shaking news. We need to figure out how this happened and see if we can find others. This is amazing. Lora, I'm very happy for you. Will you want to turn as well? If so, we need to alert the family," he said.

Just then, Rick, who was listening in but not saying anything, piped up.

"If Lora wants to go through the transition, and I can do this for her, I would be honored. However, don't we have to actually confirm I'm one of you and not some mutant vampire?" asked Rick.

Mark started howling with laughter. Falon was chuckling too.

"You're not a mutant, Rick. You cannot go and join the X-Men, sorry!" said Mark, still laughing.

"Damn!" laughed Rick. "That was a boyhood dream of mine!"

"Okay, wise guys, now what?" I asked.

"Well, now that we know, we can have fun together and be ourselves with each other. How refreshing is that?" asked Falon.

"It will indeed be refreshing and freeing," answered Rick. "I'm looking forward to Friday night."

Signing off the phone call, Rick looked at me and took me in his arms. Placing a tender kiss on top of my head, he rocked me gently.

"Hey, let's go get something to eat to replenish our energy so we can go have some more mind-blowing sex," I suggested.

"You don't have to twist my arm."

We didn't really leave the apartment that week, except for Friday. We spent all our time getting delivery, so we could spend every minute we could together in each other's arms.

Lovemaking had never felt so complete. Rick would feed me while I was lying in his arms, and that was such a sensual experience. A small bit of food, a tender kiss. Another small bit of food, then a breath-stealing, lip-bruising kiss. He knew how to play my body like a virtuoso.

Friday night, starting at the Peel Pub, we grabbed dinner and a few pitchers of beer. A live band was playing great music and we stayed there till about midnight. The four of us walked around the downtown streets because it was a beautiful spring night. In spite of the little snow on the ground, we didn't need coats, just sweaters. The guys loved us tour-guiding them around, and it was fun not having sore feet. We were in sneakers, so walking was possible.

When we got down to Dominion Square, there were a number of carriages waiting. The drivers called out to us if we wanted a romantic ride around the city.

"Oh, that would be fun. Are you guys interested?" asked Rick.

Mark and Falon looked at each other, because it brought back memories of his first time in Montreal.

"We're game," Mark said. He walked over to the horses and chose the carriage with two beautiful white horses. It was a double carriage, so four of us could go together.

"May we hire you?" he asked the driver.

"*Certaînement, monsieur*," said the driver, tipping his hat. "Blankets are on the seats inside if you find yourselves being chilled."

The four of us climbed in. Rick and I sat facing forward.

"Monsieur, can we have an extra-long ride? Perhaps around Vieux Montréal as well?" I asked.

"*Oui, madame. Avec plaisir*," he answered.

For the next two hours, the driver ushered us through all the beautiful places in Montreal. At night, it was magical with all the lights. We toured Old Montreal with the cobblestone streets, and Sherbrooke Street with all the beautiful manor houses. We went down de la Montagne with all the bistros and bars and patios, and along de la Gauchetièrre with all the modern buildings. With a little maneuvering, the carriage was able to drop us off close to where Falon had parked the car.

We thanked the driver for a wonderful ride and disembarked. Mark tipped him an extra fifty dollars and Rick did the same. Were our guys competing?

Rick took me by the waist and Mark took Falon by the hand and we walked two by two to the car.

"That was a magical night. Thank you, ladies," said Rick.

"Indeed it was," agreed Mark. "But the night is not over yet!"

"No, what else do you have planned?" I asked.

"We're going to Chenoy's!" said Mark.

"Oh, that's a nice idea," I said. "I am a little hungry. Chenoy's would settle that perfectly!"

"What's a Chenoy's?" asked Rick.

"You'll see," I said.

Piling into Falon's Mazda, Rick and I were cozy in the back. Falon pulled out into traffic and headed toward Chenoy's. It was a wonderful deli that was open twenty-four hours. It was a traditional place to grab a bite after a night out drinking and dancing. Besides, they had the best Montreal smoked meat anywhere. At the end of the night, our bellies happy, Falon dropped us off at my place with hugs and handshakes, then they went home.

Chapter 11

— Falon

Spring was here, and Mark and I had spent the winter nesting. Everyday things were done, repeated like every other weekend, and time passed. It was nice having someone to do it with. Having Mark here was so nice. We fell into a comfortable rhythm.

After the revelation last month about Rick, Lora and I had been researching supernaturals, and Olde Ones in particular. There wasn't much in human books, ancient or otherwise. However, in supernatural literature, we found quite a bit. Supernatural bookstores were hard to find, though, often disguised as occult stores that pandered to tourists, or stupid "fortune tellers" that scammed money from unsuspecting humans.

It was really too bad. Lora had a few favorite stores that were really good resources. They had connections around the world to different supernatural spots. One in particular was called the Occult Book Shoppe. This shop had a separate building that catered to real witches and supernaturals. You couldn't get in unless you knew someone, or were invited.

"Hello, Lora," said the clerk behind the front desk. We had just walked into the Occult Book Shoppe; it was not on the beaten path. You had to know it was there.

"Hi, Carmen, how are you today?" asked Lora.

"I'm doing well, thank you. What are you looking for today?" asked Carmen.

"I'm looking for information on the Olde Ones. Anything, really," answered Lora.

Carmen looked me up and down. She made a slight snarfling sound and then she smiled. Lora had told me that even though Carmen didn't look very old, perhaps in her mid fifties, she had been the "clerk" of this establishment for many years, longer than fifty. She was a member of the supernatural community, but no one knew what she was; that was a closely guarded secret. Carmen knew just about everyone and everything supernatural that went on in our city.

Carmen carefully fostered the "fortune-telling gypsy" look by wearing her gray hair up a turban and lots of flowing shawls and layered skirts with tinkling bells on it. Lora had told me had a good tourist trade in the retail store because "haunted" tours always stopped by her store.

"Your friend, I don't know her, but I sense she *is* one of us," said Carmen.

"Yes, she is one of us, Carmen. She will keep our secret. She's mated to an Olde One," said Lora.

"I have been turned," I responded, looking Carmen straight in the eye.

A quiet sucking in of her breath was the only giveaway to her surprise. Carmen considered me for a few minutes.

"I haven't heard of that happening for hundreds of years," said Carmen. "All right, I have a special collection in the back. You can look at them, but they are not for sale. Come with me."

Carmen led us to the very back of the store, which seemed unnaturally large, and then up a circular set of steps to a loft above the second-floor gallery. She pointed out two shelves with dusty old books lying flat on them.

Lora strode up to the shelf and looked at the texts. A squeal of delight indicated that she was happy with the find.

"Carmen, may I take pictures with my phone to add them to my grimoire?" she asked.

"Yes, I can share the knowledge in that way. Be aware that not all of the symbols may be photographed."

"What does that mean?"

"They will be invisible or illegible in the photo."

"Makes sense. Thank you," answered Lora.

Carmen left us alone in the loft. Lora started carrying the books over to a table. I turned on the desk light that was there to illuminate the books. It was fairly dim up in the loft.

"So how old is Carmen?" I asked.

"No one knows for sure. She's been the keeper of this store for as long as I can remember, and she never ages," answered Lora, as she looked through the books.

The first book Lora picked up was entitled *The Olde Ones: An Account of Their History.*

"This looks like a good place to start," said Lora.

"Can't we just ask Mark?" I asked.

"I was under the impression that he didn't have all that much information about the history of his people," said Lora. "Besides, we may learn something different that he doesn't know, doing our own independent research."

We spent the afternoon reading as much as we could until my eyes started hurting from the dim light. At least we confirmed what Lora knew already and what Mark had told me. Our research confirmed that the Olde Ones were not literally immortal, but their life spans were much longer than Mark thought. Some lived thousands of years, not hundreds, so the title of "immortal" seemed appropriate from a human standpoint.

We also learned that there used to be several communities of Olde Ones, and that each was possibly a different family. The book lost track of where most were, and didn't have much in the way of their family histories. *Pity!* However, they did have the whole lineage of Mark's family, so this book might belong to their family. I wondered if it was a copy, or stolen.

The book also confirmed that mortal supernatural beings like Lora were descendants of the Olde Ones who had children with humans. Only the most robust of humans could procreate with the Olde Ones, due to how they inseminated their females. The hybrids often went mad, but a few survived to also have offspring. The second generation was usually less powerful, but more stable.

We also found the recipe for the serum that was used to induce the transformation of a mortal into an immortal. Interestingly, it didn't require copulation at all, just an injection. So Mark's family had lied to him about that. All that fuss about a ceremony was just to make us have sex in front of an audience? Creepy voyeurs! They just wanted a show. Yuck.

Lora photographed that page. Some of the symbols didn't take, so she painstakingly copied the recipe into her grimoire.

"I'm going to have to go to some other sources I think," said Lora.

"Well, we did pretty good here. Just haven't looked through everything yet," I said.

"I'll come back and continue to go through these books," Lora said. "In the meantime, I'm going to look into these ingredients. Some of them I don't recognize."

We left the occult bookstore and went home. Mark was due to go away again, and I wanted to be there before he left.

Chapter 12

— Falon

Here I am in Kansas, without Toto.

When Mark left for the airport to return to Houston, his plan was to finish up the work he had there and make the arrangements for shifting the balance of his office to Montreal. We would maintain the residence in the event that we wanted time in a different place. That residence required a staff to keep it up, so he also had to make arrangements to keep them paid.

Meanwhile, at the office, my daily routine was supporting the programming staff, working on new education modules, and doing whatever the marketing people wanted me to do. The final report came in from our client in Atlanta, and Peter was pleased with the results on the work done.

"The customer is very pleased, Falon. They told us some very good things about you," said Peter once we were sitting in his office.

"Thank you. I worked really hard to keep that project on track. Sometimes it wasn't easy with all the interference we were getting."

"Oh? What kind of interference?" asked Norman. Norman Schultz was the CEO of our small software company. Together with Peter, they had built the company into what it was today.

Norman was a quiet man, and wasn't usually involved with the day-to-day stuff like Peter.

"I don't know exactly from where, but someone was countermanding some of the directions given to the programmers. The result was they would create a module that just didn't work the way the client asked for. So we ended up backtracking a few times. But it all ended well."

"That's good to know. Project management is an important skill and you have it in spades. So much so that we'd like to put your name in as project manager for the next project we are working on."

"Thank you. Where will that be? I asked.

"You'll be going to Kansas this time."

"Oh goodie—can I make Dorothy jokes?" I asked gleefully.

"Well, I don't know what kind of humor works there, but the client contact doesn't seem to have much of one. So tread carefully," said Norman.

I wouldn't be sent to Kansas until the software deal was completed. That probably meant months before I needed to worry. In the meantime, I should find a new pet sitter for the cats. I couldn't ask my neighbors anymore.

So the deal was done and it was business as usual. Traveling back and forth to work on the train was nice. I got to sit and stare out the window and not have to worry about traffic. At the end of each ride I had a ten to fifteen-minute walk to clear my head and get fresh air.

One lovely May evening going home, I had this sense of being watched, and it wasn't Mark up to his old tricks. These days, he would contact me first and let me know he was projecting to me. No, this was creepy. It started while I was walking the route from the office to Central Station. Crossing through Dominion Square, I picked up a vibe that had me checking over my shoulder.

Once I was at the station, there were so many people that I didn't notice it again, but I did when I got on the train. Eyes were boring into the back of my head. But every time I turned around there was no one there.

I was losing my mind, clearly.

By the time I got to my train stop, it was dusk. There were long shadows spreading from trees and buildings. It was a little unnerving to once again feel like I was being watched. I didn't want to act like there was a problem, because that would just alert the person if someone were watching me. I still hadn't ruled out that it was my imagination.

Purposely walking at an average rate of speed, I took a shortcut through the parking lot of a shopping mall. The street side was a little creepy but the parking lot was well lit. All through the lot I got nothing —no vibes at all—and was beginning to think I was in the clear.

Until I got to the street.

Across from me was a shadowy figure. He was tall and hooded, wearing dark clothes. He was leaning up against the building on the far side of the street. And he was looking right at me.

I pulled out my phone and called Mark.

"Hello, beautiful," he answered. "How are you?"

"Well, I'm walking home from the train and someone is following me."

"Are you all right?" came the growled question.

"So far, but he's looking right at me now. What should I do?" I asked. "Should I shadow walk?"

"Keep talking to me and start walking," he answered. "No, don't shadow walk. Never display any immortal abilities at all in public."

I did that. Looking away from the hooded figure, I started walking down the sidewalk toward our place. I was speaking loudly into my phone, even though Mark was no longer talking to me. His end had gone silent, but the call hadn't ended.

Behind me, I heard a gasp and someone yell and then a thud and a thump. I wanted to turn around and look but was too scared.

"Falon, keep walking and don't look back," came the instructions from Mark.

"Okay, hon. I'm around the corner," I said into the phone. "Should I stop and get milk on the way?"

"Don't give away that our place is close by," he hissed.

"It's not," I whispered. "There are still five blocks to go."

"Keep going, then."

I started babbling to him about stupid things—what Peter had said, what I saw on the train, what the homeless man in the park did, anything that popped into my head.

"Falon," he hissed again, "how far are you from home now?"

"About two minutes," I whispered.

"Okay, check to see if he's still behind you please," he asked.

I quickly did a shoulder check on the right. I couldn't see anyone at all, never mind the shadowy figure. Then I checked to the left, which was on the same side of the street as me. About fifty meters back, I saw someone duck into a shadow by a building.

"Um, I saw someone about fifty meters behind me," I reported.

"Damn, it didn't work," he cried. "Okay, I will try something else. When I say, I want you to run. Can you do that?"

"Yes, I suppose I can." I got ready to run by clutching my purse and briefcase in my arm instead of dangling on the shoulder strap. Luckily, I was wearing flats, so running wouldn't be impossible, just not easy.

"Go!"

I started running.

Behind me I heard a smash and a scream. I stopped and turned around to see the shadowy figure. He was crouching down close to the ground with his hands over his head screaming at something I couldn't see.

"Are you still running?" asked Mark.

"No, um, ya," I responded, as I turned and started running again. "What did you do?"

"I was able to project to his location because you were close by. Then I created a vision of a demon that threatened to devour him if he didn't turn around right then."

"I think it worked, thank you," I said gratefully.

"I wish I was home with you. I would have met you on the train."

"I'm not helpless anymore, I can fight back," I challenged him.

"You will be, but it hasn't been long enough for your body to complete all the changes. I want you safe."

"When will you be home?" I asked him.

"Not for another couple of days," was the reply.

"I can start parking my car at the train station again and driving home. It's just such a short distance. It's nice to do it in the summer."

"I know, but it's not a great area of town. I worry about you. I don't want any harm to come to my mate," he added.

"I'm walking through the front door of the building now. There is no one behind me and I cannot see anyone on the street."

"Well, I will be back to my office in about ten minutes. How about I project to you and we have a cuddle?"

"Mmmm, that would be nice. I miss you. You have to teach me these tricks. I want to be able to come to you too." I pouted.

"All in good time, my love. In good time." I could hear his smile and it warmed me. I was walking through the front door of the apartment when Mr. Paws and Scooter pounced on me with big meows and rubs.

"Ah, you're home. Good. I can hear the boys are taking care of you—that's good. Give them my hugs too."

"Mark?"

"Yes?"

"I love you with all my heart."

"I know, my love. My beautiful woman, I love you too. I'm so glad I found you again. Eternity was going to be so lonely without you."

"You say the nicest things," I purred.

Dropping my bags and the phone, I walked into the kitchen.

"Come on, boys, let's get you some dinner."

They both jumped up on the island while I was walking around it. I snuggled Scooter first; he rubbed his face against mine, purring loudly. Then I picked up Mr. Paws and he snuggled into my neck and purred like a cougar. After giving them each a hug, I put them down.

"Okay, what do you feel like having tonight? Seafood? Beef?" I asked them.

Mr. Paws answered me with a *mrrp* sound.

"Okay, seafood it is." I grabbed a can of food and split it between the two of them.

While I was spooning out the food, I was watching out the window. I spotted a figure again, leaning up against the building across the street in the shadows. I knew it was him somehow. What did he want?

I gave my boys their dinner and went to strip off today's clothes and get into something comfy for the evening. Maybe I'd take a shower? *Yeah, that's what I need.* If I was lucky, Mark would come to me while I was in the shower. *Mmmm, that is beginning to sound like a wonderful idea.*

Ten minutes later, I was standing under the stream of hot water pouring on my head. My hands were on the back wall of the shower, and I was leaning against them just letting the water sluice over my head.

That tingle that signaled Mark's astral presence started in my fingertips and zinged all along my arms down to my core.

"Hey there, beautiful lady, whatcha doing?" came the sultry Texan voice in my head.

"Mmm, waiting for you in the shower," I responded.

Immediately, I felt his presence against my back. His arms flowed around me, holding me. And I felt safe.

Mark came home later that night and found me asleep already, so he got into bed and spooned me. I woke up the next morning feeling wonderfully safe in his arms.

"Falon, I think we should install a security system," said Mark.

"Why ever for? Do you think someone is going to break in?"

"Not that kind of security. More surveillance to watch for stalkers."

"Just what would that entail?" I asked dubiously.

"Cameras, maybe a watchman."

"I don't want cameras in my home!" I said.

"Not in the home, around the home, watching the outside," he said.

"Where would you put them?"

"On the roof, looking down at the parking lot, down the balcony side of the building watching the street, and the doors. I might put a buttonhole camera in the hallway watching our floor."

"Why so many?" I asked. "Isn't it an invasion of privacy?"

"Well, in the hallway may be construed that. We can always approach the condo board and suggest these upgrades for the building. I'm sure other people in the building would appreciate the surveillance system. I could have my guy do the installation."

"Your guy?"

"Yes, I have a security company among my acquisitions. He's good too. Look, I can't go away for business and not know you're safe, or at least being protected."

"Is there really a danger from humans?"

"Probably not, but there may be a danger from my family. Don't forget I defied them."

"What would they do? Take me out?" I responded sarcastically.

"They could," he answered me seriously.

His eyes were creased with worry. He was serious. They could really come after us for bending the rules.

"We have defied them, yes, but I'm one of you now. I'm as likely to blab that as to get my legs cut off. It's my secret too now, not just theirs."

"You're right, but being careful won't be a waste."

"Okay, what will this mean? Does it mean a bodyguard?" I asked.

"Someone will escort you to and from work, just to be sure. There is no need for someone to be with you there. I'm sure you know everyone."

"That's not so bad. I was thinking you'd have him tailing me everywhere."

"No, I don't think we're there yet," he answered. "At least, I hope we aren't," he murmured.

"Do we have to have cameras inside the apartment?" I asked.

"No, just outside," he explained. "Maybe the glass doors."

"The balcony doors? We're on the fifth floor!"

"And your point is?" he asked.

"Well, who is going to come in a window five floors up?"

"Someone who is very keen on getting inside our apartment."

"That's nuts!"

"It may be, but it's a security risk. If I had my way, I'd purchase the whole building and install a major upgrade to security here," he answered.

"How much is this going to cost?"

"Nothing to you, my darling. Nothing to you."

A week later, new locks, cameras, window sensors, window film, and all kinds of things were installed in the apartment. Mark had cameras installed in strategic places on the roof, too, to monitor the grounds around the building. A LoJack was installed in my car so they could track it, and if need be shut it down. A new secure phone was given to me. I watched the workmen installing these things and shook my head.

"Who's going to monitor all this equipment?" I asked.

"Andrews' Security Company. They will be monitoring it 24/7."

They even gave me a new kind of key fob that had a tracking device in it too, and a button that I could press in the event of an emergency even if I wasn't in the car. This was some pretty fancy stuff, government or military issue, from one of Mark's companies that was a supplier. Most of this technology wasn't available to the general public yet. I hoped never to have to put any of these things into operation.

Mark supervised all the installations personally. The men couldn't leave until he was satisfied that they were complete and correct. I saw my bodyguard in passing. For what it was worth, he was a big guy, standing well over six feet. He was taller than Mark and built like a tank. I had to admit, with him around I felt very safe.

"You didn't introduce me to my tail."

"You don't need his name."

"How will I call him if I need him?"

"If you have to call him, he's not doing his job properly."

So this was my life now. I had a bodyguard but never saw him. He was supposed to be invisible so as not to spook the people I needed to deal with during the day. But it was weird.

Armand had to be programmed into the security so he could go in and feed the cats for me. That was fun to explain. But in the event we were both out of town, someone needed to do that.

Finally, the project in Kansas was about to start, and I needed to make preparations to go out of town again.

"Mark, I am leaving on Friday for Kansas City. Are you coming with me, or will you be going to Houston again?"

"I'm going to come with you for the first week or so," he answered. "There are some prospects we can look into, so it's a good opportunity. Besides, it will be nice to travel with you again. It seems like forever."

"I'll pack a suitcase for you, then."

Friday morning was bright, and we were up very early because we had to catch a 7:00 a.m. flight—that was brutal. We sat on the balcony with our coffee enjoying the perfect late spring morning and watching the sunrise—that was nice. By the time the sun was up, it was 5:15 a.m. and we had to leave.

Landing in Kansas City was a little surreal. We stopped at a rental car company and picked up a Mazda Miata that I could drive around Kansas. It would be useful going back and forth from the office to the hotel.

The drive from the airport to the hotel was fun and interesting. We put the top down and cranked the tunes. The landscape looked a lot like the West Island of Montreal: rolling hills, tree-lined streets, with brick two-story houses. It kind of made me feel at home.

The hotel my secretary had me booked in was another Holiday Inn. A no-nonsense hotel about four stories high. Nothing fancy. It didn't look as though there was anything fancy anywhere around us. Walking into the lobby, I noted the modern decor.

"Good morning, how may I help you?" asked the girl at the front desk.

"Hi, I'm checking in please. Falon, Falon Robertson."

"Yes, Miss Robertson. Do you need one or two rooms?"

"One room is fine, thank you."

"One or two beds?"

Glancing at Mark, I made a decision: "Two beds please."

Mark's eyebrows shot up in question.

"Smoking or non-smoking?"

"Oh, definitely non-smoking please."

"You'll be in room 407. You can take the elevators to your right all the way up. The room will be on your left when you get off the elevator. There is a drink machine on that floor with an ice machine as well. You can always call down to the front desk if something is missing. Our restaurant is open until 11:00 p.m. tonight. Breakfast is served all day long. I hope you enjoy your stay with us!"

Handing me two key cards, I thanked the clerk and grabbed my suitcase and walked over to the elevators, with Mark trailing after me.

"So why the two beds?" he asked me.

"Oh, that's just for the extra space to put the suitcases on," I explained.

He laughed and held the elevator door open for me while I got on. Staring at the numbers blinking on and off as the elevator ascended gave me a sense of déjà vu. Mark slipped his arm around my waist and pulled me against his body. He leaned down and kissed the top of my head.

"It's nice to be on the road again with you," he said.

I snuggled into his side. "Yes, it is. I just got a déjà vu standing here."

The door opened and we launched ourselves into the hallway looking for the room. *Nice*—it was at the end of the hall. That meant people only on one side.

Opening the door to the room, I was pleasantly surprised. It was bigger than I expected. The second bed was in a separate room. This was a suite. The windows wrapped around two sides, giving us a lovely view of the Kansas City suburbs. It was very flat. Those rolling hills weren't as noticeable from up here. What was noticeable was the fact that the horizon was a long way away. It felt as though I could see for ever.

We started unpacking suitcases, me to the dresser and Mark to the closet. I would be here for the duration of the project, which could be another six months. At least I had the same option to go home every two weeks; otherwise I'd run out of clothes. If I could find a laundromat close by, that would save me a load of time. Being away was tough on my cats though, so I needed to go home. Too bad I couldn't travel with them.

"Ready to go eat?" asked Mark.

"Almost," I answered. Mark was finished unpacking and sitting on one of the couches. "That was really fast!" I mentioned.

"I used my speed to get the job done quickly," he answered. "You can too."

"Are you using shadow walking to do things?"

"No. Shadow walking is not the same as moving at speed. As you become more adept with your new body, you will be able to do the same tasks faster and faster."

"Wow," I said. "I can do that now?"

"You should be able to do some things, yes," he said. "Try to carry a glass from here to the window and setting it on the sill. Think of running, though, instead of walking."

So I looked at the glass beside me and the window and thought of taking the glass there. I took a step and I crashed into the window. Good thing there was safety glass!

"Whoa!" Mark rushed over to pick me up off the floor. "Overshooting is a common issue when you're still learning/ We learn as children usually. Try again. This time, just think of being at the door," he said, pointing to the door of the room.

This time I concentrated on the front door to the room. I thought to myself, *Just be there now.* I took a step. The next thing I knew I was banging into the door, but not as hard as the window.

"Better," coached Mark. "Now, see yourself next to the window. Visualize it clearly in your head that you're just going to the window, then take a step."

"Okay, here goes." Again, I concentrated, this time on the window and seeing myself a foot inside it. I tried to "see" my feet on the floor a foot away from the wall. I took a step. I was there! *In a blink! Wow!*

"Oh, that was so cool!" I screamed. "I've got to do it again."

I went back to the door, bumped into it again. So I tried again. By the time I had traversed the hotel room a dozen times in different directions, I could accurately move from one place to another in one step. It was amazing.

"So what's the range of this skill?" I asked after I sat down to catch my breath. It was harder than it looked.

"Only as far as you can see, but you can see farther than you used to," answered Mark. "Short distances can be done in one step, but the farther you want to go, the more steps it requires. You can still move at superhuman speed, but it cannot be sustained very long. It requires a lot of energy."

"I can see that," I remarked, suddenly very hungry.

"Well, let's go get something to eat. I wonder if the restaurant is any good," mused Mark.

"Don't you own this one?" I asked.

"Nope."

We went downstairs and their dining room was called the Birdcage. *Cute name.* In the center of the circular room there was a giant white birdcage with all kinds of exotic birds inside. They were all talking and screeching to each other, having a good time. There was one in particular who was watching the door, and as we came in he screamed, "Someone's at the door! Someone's at the door! Get that please!"

The maître d' ran to the door to seat us.

"Nice trick with the birds," I said to him as he found us a table.

"That's Gonzo. He's a real treat, except when he starts to insult the customers' food. Unfortunately, he's a very smart bird and picks up things people say around him."

"That is fun," Mark laughed.

"Not always," said the maître d'. "We had one woman customer who took it personally."

"Oh no!" I cried. "Why would she have done that? It's obviously a bird mimicking things he's heard."

"Well, he told her she was wearing a dead animal around her neck," said the maître d', laughing.

"Was she?" I asked. "Wearing a dead animal around her neck?"

"Yes, she was," laughed the maître d'. "A stole of some kind."

He walked away shaking his head, up to the front entrance to sit some more people.

The restaurant was fairly busy for mid-afternoon. It was before dinner but after lunch, so we expected not too many people. At least there were no close adjacent visitors, so Mark and I could speak without being overheard.

The menu was interesting, with a selection of seafood and lots of beef dishes. I expected the beef dishes to be great since we were in the middle of the continent. But seafood? How fresh was it?

Mark got adventurous and ordered the curried shrimp dish. I stuck with a steak.

"Oh, that looks good," I remarked when the food arrived.

"Mmm, I'll let you know if it tastes as good as it looks. How's the steak?"

Cutting into the steak, I was happy to see they had cooked it right. It was nice and red inside, with just the outside seared.

"Looks good," I said as I stuffed a bite into my mouth. "Mmm—oh, that is good!" I said as my eyes rolled into my head with the delicious taste.

Mark took a mouthful of his shrimp and quickly reached for water as he choked and sputtered.

"Oh God, that is so over-curried it's inedible!" he cried.

"That's why I don't like curry. Especially on a delicate flavor like shrimp."

Calling over the waiter, Mark asked for the dish to be taken away, that he'd changed his mind and he would get the same as me.

"Sir, I will have to charge you for both meals," the waiter said apologetically.

"No worries, I understand," said Mark. "I just can't eat this, it's over-curried."

"I'm very sorry, sir. I will let the kitchen know."

A few minutes later another steak arrived, and it was done to perfection. Lesson learned. Don't buy seafood in the Midwest.

After dinner, Mark and I went for a walk around the outside of the hotel. It was located sort of in a suburban area without much around it in the way of entertainment or shopping. Kind of boring. So we went back into the hotel and asked at the front desk what there was to do here.

"Well, sir," said the front desk clerk, "the hotel has its own pool, spa, gym, and a number of small movie theaters that can accommodate twelve people each."

"What about shopping?" I asked. "If I need supplies, where do we go?"

"The shopping mall is about five miles away. We can easily get you a taxi to the mall if you don't have a vehicle," she replied.

"Is it a large mall or a small strip mall?" I asked.

"Oh, it's a large mall complete with a Nordstrom, a Saks, and a Macy's. So you'll be able to find all kinds of things there. Lots of boutiques and shoe stores too," she added.

"What about other restaurants?" Mark asked.

"The same road the mall is on has lots of restaurants. It's kind of like our downtown out here," she answered.

"Thank you," I said as we turned away. "Feel like taking a drive?" I asked Mark.

"Yeah, let's," he said. I hooked my arm through his and we headed for the parking lot.

"Let's put the top down, shall we?" he suggested.

Off we went. No directions, no map. *I hope we don't get lost!*

Chapter 13

— Falon

We settled into Kansas nicely. Mark got to stay a few weeks or so with me before his next trip and we took advantage of that. With his help, we explored the area and I got to know where to go. That would be useful when he was gone.

I drove him to the airport for his 6:00 p.m. flight so I could hang on to the Miata. I wasn't giving this baby back anytime soon.

"Falon, can you hold on to this for me?" he asked as he was getting out of the car. He handed me his large ruby ring with writing engraved on the inside.

"Sure, why?"

"It's bulky and I don't want it to get lost if I have to remove it at security."

"Sure," I said as I dropped it into my bag. "Have a good flight, love."

"I'll see you soon. I love you."

"Love you too!"

After I had dinner at the Birdcage, I returned to my room to watch some television or read. Mark was supposed to call as soon as he got back to the house in Houston. His flight should have been about two hours, so I expected him to call me no later than 9:00 p.m.

Glancing at the clock, I saw it was now 9:30 p.m. and I still hadn't heard from him. That started to worry me. I called the airport to verify the plane left on time. It did, and there were no delays. Neither were there any plane crashes or other emergencies. I called the Houston airport and was told the flight landed on time as well. So where was Mark?

By 10:00 p.m. I was really worried. I decided to call Gwen but got her voicemail. I called Mark and got his voicemail too. That was not good. *Maybe he didn't get on the flight?* So I called the Kansas City airport to try to find out if Mark got on the plane, but they wouldn't release that information.

I glanced at the clock again: 10:15 p.m. This was highly unusual. Not knowing what to do next, I sat on the couch and turned on the TV. Switching channels, I found the local news channel. I turned the volume down to almost nothing. By 10:30, I tried calling Mark's phone again: still voicemail. One more time I called Gwen, and this time she answered.

"Gwen speaking."

"Gwen, hello, this is Falon. By any chance, have you heard from Mark?" I asked. "I've been waiting for him to call me when he gets to the house, but he hasn't yet. I have been trying to call him, but his phone goes to voicemail. He flew into Houston this evening and he was supposed to call me when he arrived at his house."

"Hello, Falon," she answered slowly. "No, he's not here."

"Not there?" I cried. "What do you mean not there? He's not at the house? He's not at the office? He didn't arrive? What do you mean?"

Panic was starting to grip my chest.

"I don't know where he is. His flight landed but he wasn't on it," she answered.

She was not helping my panic. *What's with the cryptic answers? Why isn't she telling me anything?*

"What are you doing, Gwen? About this, I mean?" I asked her. My voice was rising the more nervous I got.

"We are currently tracing his movements," she said. "We have discovered he did not board the flight. We know he arrived at the gate and checked in for the flight, but we're having difficulty figuring out why he didn't get on the plane."

"What can I do?"

"Nothing, really. If you want to file a missing persons report with the police there in Kansas City, perhaps that would help."

"I'll do that right after I get off the phone. What else?" I asked.

"I don't know. I will keep you informed though," Gwen answered. "I've got to get back to this." She hung up. Just like that.

Oh. My. God. What has happened to him? Where could he have gone?

I called 911 and asked to speak to a police station locally.

"This is Station 57, how may I help you?" responded an officer.

"Hello, I'd like to report a missing person," I said.

"How long has this person been gone, ma'am?"

"He disappeared around 5:30 this afternoon."

"That's not long enough to declare a missing person, ma'am."

"Wait a minute—he disappeared at the airport right before he was to get on a plane to Houston. He had business meetings all day, and his sister Gwen was waiting for him."

"Ma'am, we have to wait twenty-four hours before taking a report. The person in question may have gotten drunk, or fallen asleep, or maybe hooked up with someone and missed the flight."

"No, that's impossible, all of it."

"Ma'am, most of these incidents are just that, a spouse stepping out on their spouse. I'm very sorry."

"Wait, you can't just dismiss this! Mark would never do that. I know him!"

"Ma'am, call us back tomorrow after the twenty-four-hour waiting period if you haven't heard from him yet. Goodbye."

Click.

"I can't believe it, he fucking hung up on me!" I growled. "Argh."

There was apparently nothing to do right now. I was feeling helpless, mostly because I was in a foreign country far from friends and support, and I couldn't rely on anyone here. Too uncomfortable on the couch, I turned off the TV and went to bed. I tried to sleep but I tossed all night long. All I could think about was Mark trapped somewhere. I didn't know if he was safe or in danger.

Who could have done this? He didn't just not get on the plane. Someone must have prevented him from doing it. But who? It was not like some regular thug could have taken him out in the bathroom. It would have had to be another of our kind. Someone like us who could overtake Mark. Someone in the family! *Oh no!*

Any dreams I had that night were of Mark being jumped at the airport by a member of his family, him being thrown in a large case and wheeled out of the airport, never to be seen again.

I woke up the next morning in a cold, fearful sweat. The disheveled sheets were a testament to my tossing and nightmares. I got up and ordered room service because I just didn't have the spirit to be with other people. I went to have a shower, but first I left the front door unlocked so the room service guy could bring in the food. I left them a ten-dollar tip on the table too.

A long, hot shower helped clear my mind and I felt better, but I still had this pervasive feeling that something was terribly wrong.

Putting on one of the warm robes from the hotel, I went and sat with my breakfast. It was good food and the coffee was excellent. They had brought me a whole pot.

I turned on the TV and changed the channel to get the local news.

"Last night there was a disturbance at the airport as a gentleman was apparently arrested at the gate of Flight 321 to Houston. The gentleman, identified by gate staff as Mark Chisholm, initially fought the officers when they tried to cuff him. However, police now report that the two men who took Mr. Chisholm away were fake airport officers. The police are now calling this an abduction. There are no further details about the reason for his abduction, and the police don't know any more as yet. But closed-circuit video has been pulled from the airport security which caught the incident. Here is the video."

On the screen, a low-resolution image appeared of a man arguing with who appeared to be two airport security guys. They were pushing him around and the man was letting them. When one tried to grab him, he easily avoided it by moving so fast the camera didn't see it. But when both of them leapt at him, they tackled him to the ground and wrestled cuffs on him behind his back. It looked like one of them stuck something in his neck. As they hauled the man up to his feet, it was clear he was groggy or disoriented. The two security guys dragged him away and out of the range of the camera.

"Anyone with information that can help with this investigation, please call the number at the bottom of the screen."

A phone number crawled across the screen—it was for the news station and not the police.

I decided to call the police again. "Station 57, how may I help you?"

"It's me again. I called you last night about a missing person."

"Yes, ma'am, it hasn't been twenty-four hours yet."

"I know it hasn't, but the man on the news that was attacked in the airport, Mark Chisholm, that's him."

"Oh, sorry about that, ma'am. We were only just notified by airport security around 3:00 a.m. today of that incident."

"So what are you going to do about it? That was my boyfriend, he's in danger, and I'll bet those weren't airport security."

"No, ma'am, they weren't. We've opened an investigation and are looking into it. Can I take your particulars so we can reach out to you?"

"Yes. My name is Falon Robertson. I'm living at the Holiday Inn Northeast in Kansas City, Missouri, room 407."

"Why are you in a hotel, ma'am?"

"I'm a business consultant staying for about four months."

"Okay, ma'am, I've got your particulars, so someone will be in touch. Have a good day."

"Right, thank you." I hung up the phone. Well, at least that was something. *Now what?* I thought back to the video, and how he was arguing with the guys who took him away. They ganged up on him. *Did I see them inject his neck with something?*

As my anger rose, I could feel my jaw get sore. I guess I was grinding my teeth again. I went to the bathroom and looked in the mirror. My lips looked normal. When I opened my mouth, the gums were swollen and sore. What could this be? I hoped I hadn't cracked a tooth again.

It was clear Mark was abducted. Was it for ransom? Would they call me or his family? Who other than his family would be strong enough to take him? Why would his family take him?

Maybe they were angry at us. But how would they know? I had too many questions and no answers. Pacing back and forth in the hotel room was getting me nowhere quickly. *The only thing I can do right now is wait.*

I was not a very patient woman. I caught sight of myself for an instant in the hotel mirror and my eyes were glowing red. *Huh! I'm literally seeing red.*

Chapter 14

— Mark

I came back to consciousness feeling nauseated and pained. My first thought was *how the hell did those guys know who I was at the gate?*

I was in a heap like I had been dumped as garbage. My limbs were cramped from being in a strange position for a long time. Those were the first sensations I felt. The last thing I remembered was walking away from the gate at the airport being escorted by two burly guys I hadn't recognized. Who were they?

My immediate concern was movement. Slowly, I attempted to move the different parts of my body, taking an inventory of each. All present and accounted for.

In *pain* but accounted for.

Next, I tried opening my eyes. They were gummy like I'd been asleep for too long. Rubbing my hands on my face seemed to loosen up my facial muscles, and when I opened them I couldn't see anything. I knew my hands were in front of my face, but I could see nothing.

I felt panic rising in my gut. What had they done to me?

Eventually, my immortal eyes adjusted to the dark and I started to see the outline of my fingers. *Phew, I haven't been blinded. So they have me in a dark place.*

My eyes gave off a little light, which was why I could see my hands in front of me. Good thing. Even the darkest of nights had a little light, but this place was utterly dark.

How long have I been here? "Can anyone hear me? Can somebody come and answer questions?" *I'm in a cell of some kind. A prison cell? A holding cell?*

I was not sure. I listened and heard sounds that were extremely muffled and far away.

I'm in a cell ... underground.

When I tried to stand up, my legs nearly buckled on me, but I managed. My head was swimming and I was dizzy.

Great, they gave me some kind of drug.

The longer I stood, the more the dizziness dissipated. I held out my arms as far as they could go and slowly spun in spot. I touched nothing.

"Hello!" I called out. "Is anyone there?"

Someone must be monitoring this cell. They wouldn't leave a prisoner unwatched.

Stretching my arms out as far as I could again, I tried to touch something. But nothing was within grasp.

Well, it's larger than six feet across.

I needed to figure out how big the place was. *Let's hope I'm not in a cave.*

I gingerly took a step forward expecting to bump into something. I kept my arms out ahead of me waving them back and forth. I couldn't tell if there was anything around me, and it was unnerving. For all I knew, the floor would fall off into a chasm. But I had to find out.

As I inched forward one small step at a time, I swung my arms back and forth. After five or six steps, my fingers finally brushed a surface. I took a large step, making contact with a wall.

"Is this rock?" I asked out loud. "It feels like rock. It certainly doesn't feel like concrete." I moved my fingers along the surface in different directions and discovered sharp points and cracks, divots and rough spots like you would find in natural rock. So this felt like natural rock that had been worked, mined perhaps, or just quarried, leaving a deep underground chamber.

"Hello!" I yelled again. "Anybody out there? Okay," I said out loud. "I'm underground in a cell that is over six feet square, with natural rock walls, probably the same for the floor and ceiling. Is there a door?"

Walking the perimeter of the cell, I found three corners but no door. In the middle of the fourth wall I found an opening, but it was very narrow, maybe one foot across. I estimated it was two feet off the floor and only about a foot and a half tall.

A chute of some kind? So how did I get in here? It wasn't through this opening. Besides, the opening has a grate across it, made of a crosshatch of metal rods. I must have missed something.

I walked the perimeter again, this time mapping it in my head, counting the steps to better determine size, and examining the walls closely to look for a hidden doorway.

I still didn't find a door. The rough-hewn wall gave away no secrets, and the stone was unforgiving. I punched it once to test the hardness and hurt my hand. Locating the only opening again, I went and sat on the floor opposite it. The floor was cold but it was smooth. Meaning it was manufactured. So maybe the door wasn't on the wall but on the floor?

I decided to map the floor too, starting at the wall with the opening, I worked my way from corner to corner, feeling as I went. The floor was made with slabs of material, possibly rock, but if it was it was very smooth processed rock. The surface didn't seem porous. I felt grout lines in between the slabs. I discovered a small hole in the floor in one corner—not larger than a square foot. Probably meant as waste disposal. An old odor came out of the hole, and I wasn't going to put my hand inside.

No pressure plates, no anomalies. Nothing to help. I went back to the spot opposite the "window" and sat down on the floor again.

Time passes slowly in the dark, or it doesn't pass at all. You cannot tell it's passing; there are no indicators to say it's day or night. The only "clock" you have is your body. It gets tired, it gets hungry. Those are your clock indicators.

I was starting to get really hungry. So I had been there at least eight hours. I must have skipped a meal. I felt like it was around dinner time. Whether it was or not, I had no idea.

Out of the quiet, I heard a noise. I focused on it. Someone was approaching! Were they coming to let me out?

Suddenly, a panel in the ceiling slid open across, revealing a hatch and spilling bright light into the cell. *Ah ha! That's where the door is.* A ladder dropped down.

"Get out," came a gruff male voice.

I climbed the ladder. As soon as my head crowned the opening, a bag was shoved over it. Two males grabbed me by the biceps, lifted me the rest of the way out of the cell, and put me down on the floor.

"No fighting us or we will have to tranq you again."

"Okay, I'll behave," I said.

For now anyway.

Basically dragging me so that my feet couldn't keep up, they walked me about a hundred steps, turning left and right a few times. When we stopped, they sat me down on a chair and cuffed me.

When they pulled the bag off my head, I saw I was in a room with low light. There was a table in front of me and three hooded people sitting on the far side of the table. Their faces were not visible inside the hoods.

"You may leave," said one of the hooded people, a woman. She waited until the guards had left, then turned toward me.

"State your current name for the record," said the woman.

"Current name?" I asked. *Hmm, did these people know I change my name?* "Mark Chisholm—wait, how long have I been here?"

"Mr. Chisholm, you have been detained by the council for crimes against the family," stated the woman. "How do you plead?"

"Crimes against the family? My family?" I asked.

"Yes, your family."

"What crimes have I committed? Enumerate them please, in detail," I responded. "I am not going to plead anything before I have more information about who and what this is about."

"The charges are as follows…" intoned one of the council members.

"Informing humans of the existence of our kind."

"Turning a human or attempting to turn a human."

"Withholding vital information from the council."

Okay, these charges are accurate. I've done these things. How to get out of them?

"Okay, there are mitigating circumstances. I want a representative," I said. "How long have I been here? You didn't answer my question."

"A representative will be sent to you," said the woman. "Bring in the sister."

Gwen was escorted into the chamber. It was good to see that she wasn't being held captive, nor was she cuffed.

"Gwen, he has asked for representation. You expressed a desire to assist in this matter. Will you represent him?" asked the woman.

"Yes, Councilwoman Mayer," answered Gwen. "I will represent Mark in this matter."

"You have thirty minutes to speak to your brother. We will leave you the room."

The three members of the council then stood up and exited through a door that was invisible in the back.

"Mark, you're in terrible trouble," started Gwen. "You have to tell them about Falon and give her up."

"Give her up? What the hell does that mean?" I answered. "Gwen, I'm not playing around with her. Falon is not just a human toy. She is my true love. We want to be together. How long have I been here?"

"You've been here for three days. The council would have heard your case if you had spoken before letting secrets be told. They would have vetted her and approved her turning," explained Gwen. "Now, I'm not so sure. They are very angry that you took matters into your own hands."

"Still, it's done. She is one of us, and therefore it's in her best interest to keep those secrets. She's at risk now if someone finds out the truth."

"She hasn't turned yet. The process is not complete," said Gwen. "How do you know she's strong enough to keep our secrets, Mark?"

"I know because I've seen her struggle. I know how much she's lived through. And I know how much she loves me—wait, what do you mean, 'not complete?'"

"The best we can hope for is that they'll drop these charges in lieu of her going through a test and the Turning Ceremony," said Gwen. "However, they won't let you do the Turning."

Mark growled deeply. "No one touches my Falon but me. Especially someone who has to inseminate her for the Turning."

"You may have no choice."

"I will never let them know her."

"You forget, I know her. I've met her, and I know where she is right now," threatened Gwen.

"You would do that? You would betray me like that?" I was getting angry now. My fangs were descending.

"I would for the family, yes."

"What kind of a sister are you?"

"I'm not really your sister, Mark. You were told that because I raised you. We have different parents."

A knock on the door announced the council returning to the chamber. I was thinking hard about what Gwen had just revealed—surprised, yet not surprised.

"Have you convinced your brother to plead?" asked the councilwoman.

"No, I'm afraid not, Councilwoman," answered Gwen. "But he has a request for the council to consider."

"What is that?"

"That the council grants that his human be given the test for the Turning."

"To what end?"

"He claims they are true love mates and want to be together. If she can turn, then she will be held to our laws and our secrets."

"Guards, return this prisoner to his cell while we deliberate on this request."

"As you wish, Councilwoman."

Two guards stepped up, bagged my head, uncuffed me, and marched me back to the cell. This time, I walked down the ladder rather than being thrown unconscious.

What seemed like a day passed before I heard the guards coming back.

"Here is some food," said a voice from above. The panel slid across and a tray was lowered into the cell. Just enough light came through the ceiling that I could find the tray and eat. It was a spartan meal: bread, meat, apples, cheese. Better fare than I expected, really. A little while later, the tray lifted up and the panel slid closed.

"So much for that light," I mumbled. I was worried about Falon. She would be going out of her mind not hearing from me for this long, especially since I would have called her when I landed in Houston. *What is she doing right now?*

This was all my fault. I was the one who decided to pursue her. I was the one who couldn't stay away, and now she was in danger. I had expected it, but not this quickly. I had hoped we would have had a little time to make a plan and escape.

Falon had wanted to stay with her career though. Understandable, but I should have told her why she couldn't. *What will she do?* My thoughts were all over the place. I contemplated what Falon would do. She might have called Gwen. *That's why Gwen knows where she is!* Would she have called the police? They wouldn't do anything for a couple of days either.

In the middle of my musings, the panel in the ceiling slid open again and a ladder dropped.

"You've been called back to the council."

Climbing the ladder, I knew what to expect this time. I cooperated until they took me around the first corner. Then I fought like a hellion to shake their grasp. Swinging my weight to one side, I crashed one of the guards into the wall. A satisfying sound of air whooshing out of his lungs let me know he was incapacitated a little.

One hand free, I swung it at the second guard with all my strength. My fangs descended and I leapt onto the guard and bit down as hard as I could into the second guard's shoulder. That guard was down, but the first one I'd knocked into the wall was back up on his feet. I grabbed his chin and threw his head backwards into the same wall. It made contact with a sickening bone crunch; not enough to kill him. He started shaking the stars out of his eyes, I grabbed him by the arm and delivered a bite to his bicep. Again, the venom rendered the guard unconscious.

Not really knowing where I was, I started running down one of the halls. At least my vision was adjusting to the low light levels. I passed several doors that didn't appear to go anywhere. At the end of the hall, there was a set of stairs going up.

Good, maybe I can find an exit.

I was just about to get through a door at the top of the stairs when a tranquiliser dart hit my thigh. I pulled it out quickly, but it had already delivered its payload.

I crumpled to the floor in a heap.

This time when I woke up in the cell, my head was bleeding and the pain in my shoulder told me that I'd basically been dropped down here. My shoulder felt dislocated, my skull seemed to be fractured, and maybe a leg too.

With great difficulty, I managed to manipulate my useless arm in order to pop the shoulder back in place. Pain surged through my body, completely waking me up. There wasn't anything I could do about the head injury, but I carefully felt along my lower left leg and found the fracture. This one wasn't all the way through, so if I sat straight and still, it should heal correctly. I ripped a sleeve from my shirt and wrapped it very tightly around my leg to support it as much as possible. My immortal body would heal, but I didn't want the fracture to heal badly.

The total darkness was like a dampening blanket. It depressed everything. My efforts to produce endorphins for myself didn't work. Thinking of Falon in her sexy black lingerie helped, but my pal knew she wasn't close by and didn't want to play.

"Thanks a lot, you little schmuck. I could have used the painkillers," I said to my cock. "Where are you when the going gets tough, eh?"

Sometime later, what felt like days perhaps, the family took another try at getting me to spill the truth. This time they promised me I didn't have to give up my secrets or "my humans," but they needed to know who she was.

Why were they so interested in who Falon was? I wasn't giving them anything.

I don't trust them. And yet it's just me here. Clearly they knew where we were, and my schedule to be able to abduct me.

They tortured me to near death, then let me heal over and over again. When I was exhausted, they injected me with venom to revive me and heal the wounds. They wouldn't let me go and they wouldn't let me die. I'm not sure, but I think this went on for a week or so. They hadn't been back for a long while though, perhaps a couple of days. It was difficult to judge time in the dark, but I'd been fed twice since the last beating.

I lay there on the floor of the cell exhausted, knowing that the pain would disappear and the wounds would heal, all to happen again. I could hear Gwen's voice speaking to someone above me. She was pleading on my behalf that I and the human had true love like she'd never seen before.

Someone slapped her across the face and I heard Gwen cry out and fall to the floor. The elders didn't believe in true love. Probably because it hadn't happened in so long.

I feared I would have to admit that I had tried to turn her already, that I gave her the bite and that she had started to show signs of turning. That would be the only thing that would end this.

The next time I heard the guards coming, I prepared myself. They were better prepared too, but this time I was being taken to the council chamber. I didn't fight them.

"Mr. Chisholm, you have been quite uncooperative," spoke the councilwoman.

"Gee, I thought the guys wanted to do some line dancing."

"Your sarcasm will not help you here, Mr. Chisholm."

"Will anything?" I asked

"Yes, your answers."

"Well, I guess you're going to be torturing me again," I said, but my conviction to stand against them was gone. I had decided to answer their questions.

"How long have you known the human?" asked another council member.

"Her name is Falon. I've known her since 2016," I replied.

"Since 2016, you say? Weren't you in a previous persona at that time?"

"Yes, I was a Greek man in Montreal at that time."

"Have you been in contact with her all this time?"

"No. I left her a year later, well almost a year later. On orders from my father."

"Why didn't you stay away?"

"I did. But seven years later, she just walked into my life again. I tried to stay away, but it was just not possible. It seemed fated. Why else would we have happened to be in the same place twice?"

"So what did you do when you saw her the second time?"

"I watched."

"Just watched?"

"No, it drove me mad not to go say hello. She didn't recognize me of course, but I went to talk to her. The same chemistry was there. As soon as I got close to her, I could smell her. My body knew her, and my body responded."

"Did you have sex with her then?"

"No! We were in a restaurant. But I wanted to, I needed to. I needed her like I needed air. I managed to control myself though and said goodnight to her."

"You didn't have sex, so then how did you end up together?"

"Well, I ran into her the next morning, we had breakfast together, and she gave me her number."

"And then what?"

"Well, I tried to forget about her. But I dreamed of her every night. Her scent, her hair, her body. I remembered loving her all those years ago. My desire for anyone else evaporated. The girls I had dates with, I canceled, because they couldn't hold a candle to Falon. I knew she was my one true love."

"When did you tell her about us?"

"Oh, not for a long while. I made arrangements to be where she was so we could run into each other. It was quite obvious, I thought. But I had hurt Falon so deeply that I had to gain her trust. At the same time, I was so conflicted that I kept telling her to see other guys, to indicate it was casual. But I hated every lie. It wasn't casual for me. Every time she was with someone else, I could smell them on her and it made me crazy. I found myself doing things to claim her as mine. I bit her during lovemaking."

"Was this during insemination as well?"

"Yes, it was. I must confess, I wanted to plant a child in her belly so much. I wanted her to have my son."

"Were you aware that biting during insemination would lead to the change?"

"No, at that time I did not. I tried not to bite her, but I could no longer stop myself from doing that. The best I did was make sure it didn't give too much venom."

"When did you explain to her what you were?"

"That happened partially when I left her the first time, and then somewhat after I bit her. I felt I had to tell her the truth. I didn't know if she would turn and that would scare her."

"Did she turn?"

"I watched for signs, but there were none. So when I realized that she wouldn't turn, I consulted with Gwen to find out what it actually took."

"Is that when you decided to turn her?"

"That was when I decided to give her the choice."

"And what happened next?"

"I explained to her fully who I was, what I was, and that she could join me. It took a lot of explaining, because she thought I was nuts. Eventually showing her how we heal worked. When she told me that she loved me with all her heart, I was the happiest man on the planet. But she was very angry with me, and that would take time to get over."

"So you still didn't have the Turning?"

"No. That only happened in August last year—I'm not sure what today is."

"So you got consent, you had sex, climaxed, and inseminated her fully, and delivered a full dose of venom at the same time?"

"Yes, in a nutshell. The experience left me feeling like a human, I was so weak. Falon was unconscious for a day or two. I was scared because I didn't know what was supposed to happen."

"Of course not. This is usually done under the supervision of a doctor, to be able to handle complications. It was truly stupid of you to undergo this attempt without the family present to witness and protect you and her," said the councilwoman angrily.

"You put her life in jeopardy by acting without consideration!" she shouted. "You put our lives at risk by acting without our consent!" Then, after collecting herself, the councilwoman asked, "Have there been any outward signs that she is turning?"

"Well, she didn't die," I said, chuckling. "Beyond that, I did a cut test after a few days, and it healed quickly—not instantly, but quickly. So I figured the change must be started."

"Her life is still at risk," said the third councilwoman. "Without the serum we give them, the process will not finish successfully."

"I didn't know this," I said quietly. "What do you propose, then?"

Chapter 15

— Falon

It had been about two weeks since Mark was abducted. The police hadn't done anything at all. They wouldn't answer my calls, and neither would Gwen. I was at my wit's end.

All the while, I continued to work. Luckily, we were only just in the start-up phase, which meant attending basically mindless meetings during which the customer explained what they wanted and the programmers didn't listen. I had to take notes so that I understood the customer's point of view. I recorded the sessions, which was very helpful. That way I went back over the meetings and pulled out key points.

I was doing this in my hotel room because it was quiet and I didn't get interrupted. I was trying to focus, but my mind kept drifting to Mark. The last time we were in the room together he was showing me how to do that speed-walking thing he does.

Someone knocked on my door. I got up and did the speed-walk to the door, almost running into it, but managed to stop myself in time. Looking through the peephole, I saw two uniformed police outside.

I opened the door and invited them in. "What can I do for you, Officers?" I asked.

"We are following up on a missing persons report you made about two weeks ago," replied one of the officers.

"Really? You're only now looking into a person being kidnapped at the airport?"

"We had a lot of eyewitness testimonies to sift through from that event. There were a lot of people sitting in the departure lounge at the time of his abduction. But as you may understand, everyone saw something different."

"So why are you talking to me now?" I asked.

"You stated that you were his girlfriend?"

"Yes, that's right," I said.

"Except his family doesn't know anything about you, is all."

"Oh, ya, that."

"Um, what does that mean, Miss?"

"Mark's family is very particular—they're very rich, you see, and don't approve of me. So Mark and I haven't told them about us."

"We spoke to a Gwen Mitchell, who claims to be his sister. Do you know her?"

"I've met her once. I didn't know her last name," I answered.

"She said she met you, but that you were an employee of theirs?" asked the cop.

"When she met me, I was sort of an employee. It was back in Atlanta, Georgia. I was a consultant with a software company that was installing a large project there. Gwen's company happened to own the company that was our client. I hadn't known that at the time, though."

"Do you still work for them or any of their companies?" asked the cop.

"Not that I am aware of. The company I work for is a software company from Montreal, Canada. I'm in Kansas City with another project for us, and my position here is project manager."

"When was the last time you saw or spoke to Mr. Chisholm?" asked the cop.

"That morning. We got up, had breakfast, packed a suitcase and I drove him to the airport for his flight that afternoon. He was supposed to call me when he got to the office in Houston to let me know he landed safely."

"So the last time you saw him was at the gate?"

"No, it was where I dropped him off at the door of the airport. I didn't park and go in with him as I was on my way into work."

"Did you see Mr. Chisholm speak to anyone outside the airport?"

"No, not that I noticed. He went right inside and I pulled away from the sidewalk. I really wasn't watching him but looking for cars."

"When was the first moment you thought something was wrong?" asked the cop.

"I had an uneasy feeling when he was thirty minutes late calling me. I called the Houston house. Gwen answered. She hadn't heard from him either, and that's when I started to get really worried. It was around then that I heard the report on the news, and recognized Mark in the video from the airport. I called the police immediately."

"Did you recognize the people attacking Mr. Chisholm in the video?"

"No, I didn't. But the video was not of great quality when they aired it. They must have downgraded the quality, because I'm sure the CCTV footage would have been better."

"Does Mr. Chisholm have any enemies that you know of?"

I had to think about this question for a minute. Did I tell them about the family? I was not supposed to let that secret go.

"Not that I can think of. He may have business competitors that don't like him, but he's never mentioned enemies per se."

"Finally, how long have you two been a couple?" asked the cop.

"Officially? Since last August. We dated and saw each other on and off before that."

"Thank you, Miss Robertson. If we have any other questions, we'll be in touch."

With that, the two cops turned around and left without another word. Now what was I going to do? I had the distinct feeling Gwen wasn't telling me everything. I didn't tell them that, but I felt she was withholding.

Oh, Mark, I hope you're okay. I'm so worried about you. Please come back to me.

The next day, I tried calling Gwen again and the office in Houston. Gwen was a no-answer, but I got Mark's assistant on the phone. He told me that the police were following up down there too. They thought it was a kidnapping for money, but no one had received a phone call demanding a ransom yet.

I had to stay focused on the project I was managing. I had an extremely difficult week. While we made progress documenting the process for the customer, the programmers were being babies. "We can't do that"—well, figure out what you can do, twerps! Of course I couldn't say that to their prissy little faces. *Argh!*

The first part of the process was documented, diagramed out, and in the hands of the programmers to come up with a first module of the software. It built on modules that we already had, so they just had to tweak the parameters and customize the screens.

Hopefully, we'd have something to walk through in a couple of weeks.

I followed up with the police a couple of weeks later to find out if anything new had been uncovered. The detective in charge spoke with me, but his report was very discouraging.

"Miss Robertson, I don't know what to tell you. Mr. Chisholm has disappeared off the face of the planet. No one here or in Houston can find a trace of him. There has been no ransom demand and no body found. We are stuck. Until there is new information, this case has been put on hold. I wish I could give you better answers. Perhaps he's just run off. Men do that sometimes. He's probably sitting on a beach somewhere sipping a mai tai."

"No, that's not right, he wouldn't just leave me without saying something," I cried. I was close to breaking down. I could feel the stupid tears collecting in my eyes ready to betray me. I sounded like some chump wife whose cheating husband had just run off with a bimbo.

"I'm really sorry, Miss," he said regretfully.

I had no choice. There was nothing they would do, and there was nothing I could do. Down deep in my bones, I knew it was the family. But I couldn't say anything. Again, I found myself asking that stupid question: *What am I going to do?*

Well, one thing was for sure. I was going home for the weekend. I'd better start packing.

Chapter 16

— Falon

My support system was Lora. She was my rock; she set me straight when I was all twisted up. I could bounce ideas off her and she'd tell me if I was being stupid. She hugged me and rocked me when my heart was broken.

Lora was the one who helped put me back together again.

It was a little over four weeks into the Kansas City project by the time I went home for a weekend to do laundry, pet my cats, and see my friends. This time I was coming home in the middle of a crisis.

As soon as I landed in Dorval, I called Lora to let her know I'd arrived.

"Falon, good, I'll be there in an hour," said Lora.

"Okay … just to let you know, I had a rough couple of weeks down there."

"What happened?" asked Lora.

"Mark has been abducted," I said, barely keeping it together.

Getting home, I knocked on Armand's door first. When there was no answer, I took out my spare key and went into the apartment. I was immediately assaulted by that wonderful odour of unclean cat boxes. Yuck!

"I have to hire a pet sitting service. I think I've overused my neighbor," I thought out loud.

"Hey, boys, how ya doing?" I got down on the floor and hugged them both because they were both on my lap. They wouldn't get off, so they were lonely.

"Let's go get you some dinner, shall we?" They both ran into the kitchen, sat down, and meowed. When I got there, the dry food was empty and the water was almost dry. It was a good thing I left the toilet open—they will drink from a clean bowl if necessary.

"Someone hasn't been looking after you, have they? I am sure there is a really good explanation." I walked over to Armand's place and knocked on the door.

"Hullo, Falon, you're back?" asked a sleepy voice.

"Yes, Armand, I'm back. Listen, no judging or anything, but have you been doing the cats every day?"

"Ah, no. I go every two days, because it's usually not a problem. Today was the day I would have gone in."

"Oh, I see. Well, to let you know, they were out of food, the water bowl was dirty, and the box was disgusting. Look, I've asked too much, so I'll hire a sitter next time, okay?"

"No, I can do it. I want to. I just got busy this week. Sorry."

"Okay, well, I've got to unpack and do laundry. So, bye."

Back in my apartment, I opened a can of food and divided it up into two bowls and put them down on the floor for the cats. They tucked into the food—meaning they were quite hungry. Next, I had to do something about that smell. I opened up all the windows in the apartment and got a good cross breeze flowing. That would clear out the stink quickly. Now, for the least fun part: changing the litter.

"I'm just going to toss the whole damned thing. Easy!" I had a brand-new bag of litter, so I grabbed a large garbage bag, dumped the old litter completely. I cleaned out the box with some Pine Sol—love that stuff—and filled it up with nice clean litter. *Sigh. Smells much better now.*

Then I started doing things robotically: unpacking, putting things away, and separating my laundry. When the door buzzer went off, I knew Lora had finally arrived. I buzzed her through and left my door open.

"I'm here!" Lora called out when she walked in and shut the door.

"How does it smell here?" I asked her.

"Okay, nice to see you too. That was a strange greeting," she responded.

"Oh, sorry, oh it's so good to see you again!" I went over and gave her a big hug.

"It smells okay," Lora said. "Was there a problem?"

"Yup. The cats hadn't been fed, the water had dried up, and the box hadn't been cleaned. When I walked in here it smelled like a garbage dump."

"Wasn't Armand looking after the cats for you?" she asked.

"Yes, but he was asleep when I arrived, so I don't know the story." I was a little miffed. "He says he comes in every two days. I don't know though, it looked longer than that."

"He's been acting strangely the last couple of weeks," said Lora.

"Really?" I asked. "How so?"

"He hasn't wanted to babysit for me, always busy, secretive, doesn't answer his phone," she explained.

"That's not like him. Do you suppose he has a girlfriend?" I asked.

"A real one?" she giggled. We both had the same problem with him. He was so desperate for a girlfriend he kinda pretended we were it. He was a wonderful man—loyal, gentlemanly, honorable. He just wasn't my type, and he wasn't Lora's type either. But that didn't stop him from trying.

"Perhaps," she concluded. "It would explain some things. Here, let me help you with that."

Lora came and helped me sort and start the laundry. It was nice having an extra pair of hands there. We chatted about what was going on in her life and what was happening at the office she worked at. It was an organization that helped women escape their abusive lives and find shelter. They had the office in a regular building so it wouldn't be obvious. There had apparently been an uptick on the number of women coming in looking for sanctuary. There didn't seem to be any explanation, but it was putting a serious strain on their resources. Her kids were all good. Their father had taken them for the weekend last week, giving her some needed time off. Their father was a jerk, but he was okay with the kids.

"Now that we've been through all my life the past month, tell me the whole story about what has happened to Mark?" asked Lora.

"Our trip to Kansas City started blissfully. We got to spend some quality time together. Then he had to go home to Houston. But he never got there."

"What do you mean he never got there? Where did he go?"

"I don't know," I said. "He was kidnapped at the airport—their security video caught the whole thing—and has disappeared. Two large men dressed in airport security uniforms dragged him from the gate. I think they tranquilized him too. It was on the news in Kansas. The police down there have nothing. It wasn't for ransom. I've received no calls, so they called it 'he left his life' as a reason."

"I don't buy that," said Lora. "That doesn't sound like him at all. If he had to leave you, he would have told you, like before."

"Before?" I asked her.

"When he was Zisis."

"Yes."

"Lora, the police are telling me he's just left—like run away. I don't know what to think. I'm worried about him. I suspect his family is behind this abduction, but there isn't anything I can do."

"That's not possible," she said confidently. "When I looked into him, I saw the truth of his love. It was pure. There were no qualms, no hesitations, no questions. That man is so completely in love with you, he would sacrifice himself to be with you. Don't you doubt him."

"When was that?" I asked her.

"The first time we met," she said. "I felt something very special about him. And you know me, I can't help poking the dragon. I had to find out. It was easy to collect what I needed when we danced." Lora's eyes were sparkling with mischief.

"So you think he's okay?" I asked.

"No, I didn't say that. I said he hasn't left you." Lora pondered something for a moment. "I don't know if he's okay, but perhaps we can find out."

"What do you need?"

"Let me consult my grimoire. There must be a ritual I can do to find him, or at least to be able to see him."

She went to her laptop and opened a fancy-looking document. She started going through pages.

"Your grimoire is on your computer?" I asked.

"Of course it is!" she exclaimed. "And on my phone too. How else can I carry it around with me everywhere in case I need it?" She smiled.

"While you're doing that, I'm going to start dinner for the two of us. Is pasta okay?"

"Hon, anything you cook is fantastic, so I'm not fussy," Lora responded.

I got busy in the kitchen, taking out the ingredients for a basic sauce. I didn't have any fresh vegetables I needed.

"I'm running out to the store across the street. Do you want wine with dinner?"

"Oh boy, yes please!" she answered.

Next door was a *depanneur*—or a corner store—that had everything you need in life. It had a small green grocery section where I got some peppers, onions, tomatoes, and chillies, and an extensive section for wines. I picked out a decent Chianti to go with dinner. They also had packages of lean ground beef. Excellent, I could make a nice meat sauce. I couldn't help getting a baguette too. It was more starch, but so what!

Back at home, chopping veggies was relaxing. A normal thing to do that quieted my mind. I reflected on what Lora and I had learned about the Olde Ones. Was it true that maybe Mark was older than he said? Why would he keep that from me? It didn't really matter.

Pulling the ground beef out of the package, I broke it up in a skillet, adding a healthy spoonful of chopped fresh garlic, thyme, oregano, parsley, sage, and rosemary. I let that simmer until it was all brown and stirred in the onions and other veggies. Once all the mixture was sizzling nicely, I blended the basic sauce, chopped tomatoes, and paste in a large pot. Adding in the meat mixture thickened it up nicely. I let it simmer on low until the pasta was cooked and drained.

Scooping up large servings of the sauce, I poured it over the plate of pasta—this time fusilli—and topped it off with fresh parmesan cheese. I took the plates out to the table and went back for glasses, cutlery, and the wine. Lastly, the baguette with some cream cheese to make it a gastronomic experience.

"Dinner's ready!" I called Lora. "Coming!" she replied. "Yum, it smells wonderful. Thank you for cooking."

"So what did you find?" I asked once we were seated and the wine was poured.

"I found a spell that will let me see him if he's alive, if you have an object that means something to him."

I thought about that. *Did I have something with me?*

"Just a moment," I said as I got up from the table. I checked my purse, and there in the bottom of it was his ring, the big bulky thing that he took off at the airport because he didn't want to lose it at security. "Will this work?" I asked her.

"That'll do nicely," she answered.

After dinner, she collected a number of items. She gathered them all up and took them to the balcony. Filling the large shallow bowl with water, she murmured an incantation, then she dropped some white sage and some sweetgrass in the water. Continuing to speak low, she finally took my hand and placed Mark's ring in the bowl in the very center.

An image started coalescing in the water. It looked like a reflection, but it wasn't from the outside. It was a dark room. The water had tiny ripples on the surface, making the image fade in and out. Lora spoke some more words and the ripples calmed down. She waved her hand over the water with my hand in hers. I felt a tingle of her magic power zing my hand as it passed over the bowl.

Finally, the water settled into an image of Mark sitting in a dark room. His hands were tied to a chair; he faced three people across a long table. They were all wearing hoods. But you could see their eyes glowing a reddish color. They looked truly scary. One of the three hooded figures was speaking but we couldn't hear any sound. Two others, appearing to be guards, roughly pulled Mark to his feet and dragged him out of the chamber. That's where the vision stopped.

"Well, he's alive," said Lora. "That's good. But it appears he's a prisoner somewhere. Do you recognize anything? Can you communicate with him like he does with you?"

"I don't recognize anything," I said. "He hasn't taught me how to communicate like that yet. I can try." I closed my eyes and tried to focus on Mark's face. I was willing myself to see him, but only static came through. I tried to hear him and tried to hear beyond what my ears could hear. Nothing.

"I just don't know how," I said, defeated. "While I cannot recognize anything, I can guess though … that they are part of the council of elders he spoke to me about."

"Tell me, can you still feel his heartbeat?" she asked

"Yes, I can."

"That is your answer, then. As long as you can feel his heartbeat, you are connected, true love mates, and both alive," Lora explained. "Keep focusing on that."

I looked into the eyes of my best friend. I saw sadness there too. Being a member of the supernatural world, she understood what it meant for me to become an immortal.

"You won't always have me around," said Lora. "Eventually, you will need to leave, change your lives."

"That's not going to happen anytime soon," I assured her. "Besides, you've got an option now, with Rick." Then I hugged her because she was like my sister and I loved her as much as I loved my brothers.

I will not give up on Mark. He will return to me.

Chapter 17

— Lora

Falon left for Kansas. She would be there for about six months again, with visits back home once a month. I wanted to be ready for her when she got back the next time.

We found a lot of information at the occult bookstore before she left, but it still wasn't complete. I needed to find another source that was a family history. Perhaps if I looked up my family tree again, I could trace that family to another book.

Why was I doing all this? Well, Rick needed to know who he was. And I wanted to make sure we weren't part of the same bloodline—I doubted it.

I wonder if our DNA could give us any information? I should get blood samples from all four of us. Mark's would show the DNA of his family; Rick should be different. Falon should be different again because she's a human turned, and I was a human hybrid.

A phone message was left at my office. Carmen had found another possible book for me. I would go to check it out tonight.

After work, I took the train downtown and got off in Chinatown. Carmen's bookstore was in a little back alleyway and the door was hidden from the street.

A bell rang as I opened the door. "Hello!" I called out.

"Lora, I'm glad you could come. I have something very interesting for you. Come see."

She brought me to a table in the back, but still in the main part of the bookstore. I still always got the feeling that the store was much larger inside than it was outside.

"Carmen, is your store condensed? It looks very small on the outside, but inside it seems to go on forever," I asked her.

Chuckling, she looked at me and winked. "Lora, my dear, it's magic," she said mysteriously.

I should have guessed I'd get that answer.

"Here! The book I found for you—isn't it grand?" she asked.

I sat down in front of the book. The title was *Families of the Olde World from Days Gone Bye*. It certainly looked like it would help. Opening the pages, it was filled with entries of births, deaths, marriages, and things like that. It was like a city or a church register. Wonderful information. But it wasn't indexed. It would take weeks to go through the information.

At least the book seemed to be organized by village or community, and then entered sequentially. Perhaps I would be able to find Mark's name in it. I'd need to know his original name to do that.

"Carmen, may I borrow this book and take it with me?" I asked.

"I don't know, Lora. Who are you looking for?" asked Carmen.

"Actually, I'm not looking for anyone specific, I'm just doing research on my family tree. But I will need to decipher this book to find the appropriate entries before I can go backwards. It will take time," I explained.

"I guess you are correct, so yes, you may borrow it. Shall we say a week at a time? If you need it longer, you will have to let me know," she suggested.

"I think a week is fair. Thank you, Carmen. Any other new books?"

"I've picked up the Dom Sapoza grimoire. It is going to be an interesting read. And I found an odd little book. It doesn't qualify as a grimoire, but it has spells in it. Some sort of notebook. But it is terribly old. I want to determine how old it is before putting it on the shelf."

"Can you carbon date this book?"

"I don't actually know," said Carmen. "It's a laborious process and few places have the equipment to do it. However, I have a friend in the archaeology department at UNB, and he may be able to help me. I would love to know how old this one is."

"It does look like it's about the Olde Ones, so maybe it's contemporary to them?" I asked. Picking up the book, I gathered my other things and bid her goodbye. I had another store I wanted to stop by that dealt in the occult as well, and perhaps they had something. It was still early afternoon, so I had time to spend a couple of hours there. Maybe I would strike paydirt.

In an out-of-the-way place downtown, basically behind three buildings, and not on a street, was a door that led to a magical store. It had no name; it was simply known as the occult store. It catered to people like me. We weren't common, but not that rare. Supernaturals weren't restricted to "local" shopping. We could go anywhere. So the location of the shop didn't really mean anything.

Walking through the doorway meant you walked into another dimension. The shop existed outside of our reality. It was dim in here too, but that was to protect all the very old items inside. Light was harmful.

Inside, it was very messy and disorganized. There were books everywhere and paraphernalia littering the surfaces and floors. It looked like no one had been there in a very long time.

"Esperanza, are you here?" I called out.

"Si, who is asking?" was the answer, from a disembodied voice.

"Lora O'Reilly."

"Come on inside, Lora O'Reilly. How may I help you?"

A shield was dropped and I could see the interior of the shop clearly. It looked different now. It was neat and orderly. Books were all on the shelves, and tables were clear of debris. Nice illusion.

"I'm looking for information about the Olde Ones. Hopefully about my ancestors," I said.

A ball of soft white light appeared halfway up from the floor at my waist.

"Follow the light, please," said the voice.

As the light began to move, it swerved and dodged around objects on the floor. I followed it as quickly as possible.

It led me through a maze of shelves of books, ladders, cases that displayed occult objects, and so many other bizarre things. Some of them I couldn't identify. Some of them I didn't want to. The spotlight was zipping quickly, so I had no opportunity to look at anything anyway.

It stopped in front of an old piece of furniture that sort of looked like an armoire. I didn't know if this was where I was supposed to look or not. Either way, the light had vanished. It was very dim back here, wherever "here" was.

"The armoire contains our entire collection on the Olde Ones. If it is not here, then I doubt you can find it anywhere," said the disembodied voice.

A click sounded and the door to the armoire opened, revealing a very large collection of books. The interesting thing was the armoire was not an armoire, but a doorway to a room. Walking into the room, the lights grew brighter so that I could actually read the titles on the books' spines packed along the walls on shelves.

A circle of light illuminated a round table in the very center of the room. I put down my bag and walked over to one shelf and started reading titles. I was looking for genealogies.

On my fourth stack, I found books about the genealogy of some families. I grabbed the first one and went back to the table to read. The book was in incredible condition, like it was created in the modern era, not some ancient time. I cleaned my hands with a wet nap to make sure there were no oils on my fingers and waved them to dry before picking up the book.

There was an "onion skin" transparent sheet left in between the pages with a cipher on it. It seemed to line up with four points on the page, and when I overlaid it that way, suddenly I could read the text. That was magic! Going from an ancient language to English with just a cipher? *Who am I to complain?*

I was shocked when I started reading the first page. The dates were eons before the modern era. In fact, it looked like they predated the Sphinx of Egypt. Now the common accepted age of the Sphinx is about 4,500 years old. However, there is evidence that it may be much older than that, as many as 12,000 years. The face it has now was carved from a different original face, and the weathering indicated a much older monument too. Either way, this book predated that by some 10,000 years! The people who kept these records used a very different dating system. It was only as someone subsequently translated some of the dates that I was able to make sense of it.

Reading through the pages, I discovered that the original author had sought to record the history of his/her family. The story they told was quite fascinating. There were many clans of people, all descendants of people who came from the stars.

Their home planet had become unstable and they had to find a new home.

They had discovered Earth about 33,000 years ago, which they called Arvidan. When they arrived, the only people they found were very primitive humans. These humans were mostly hunter/gatherers.

There had been lush forests and vast water supplies, with lots of game. Primarily meat eaters, the aliens were delighted that there were lots of animals and that the atmosphere was ideal for them. They made a decision to live far away from the native people, and only hunt for food on the other land masses. This was possible using their ground vehicles, which could hover.

"We were from the planet Zydees and we called ourselves Zydeans. We'd been on this planet long enough that it had been decided that we should spread out and seek out more people, perhaps with the goal of species integration, or at the very least to bring in fresh blood to our people. There were thirty-five groups assigned thirty-five locations around the globe. The group of this story was destined to go to what is now Oregon (translation). *As they migrated north, they settled in different areas, learned more of the planet, and the people in each area.*

They made contact with primitive humans and showed them how to cook their food to get more nutrition out of it. Their hope was to advance humanity until they were compatible with themselves so that they could refresh their DNA.

As they traveled northward from the southernmost continent, toward their final destination just south of the ice sheet, they encountered different groups of humans—each at a different stage in development. They saw some of the skills they taught the earlier people were adopted and passed on to descendants.

Eventually, the human populations were advanced enough to intermingle with them. The first pregnancies the humans had from our men were multiple births, both dangerous to their females, and considered a "gift from the gods." These couplings were sought after by the humans. Male humans participated as well, giving our women some success in childbirth. Those children were born immortal and kept with us.

In one such village, the people held lotteries to determine who would get to lie with one of our people. In another, they wanted us to teach all the young adults how to copulate so that it was pleasurable. Their high priestess insisted that first time girls be with one of us.

In some villages, the children born of couplings with us were treated with suspicion, and in others they were treated like demi-gods. Almost all of these villages thought we were gods, and this eventually became the reason we stopped contact.

The span of time between these encounters varied from a few hundred to thousands of years. We kept in contact with our other groups, and learned they all had similar experiences with humans. Group 32 became quite entwined with the humans in their area.

Consistently, we observed that the mixing of our DNA with the humans' DNA caused several outcomes: the child had a longer lifespan; they had a more robust physical body. They often manifested skills such as magic. And they became people of authority in their villages.

They learned skills from us so that their villages could stop roaming and create farmland. They developed more tools to work with and harnessed the power of some of the animals they encountered.

We also observed that the children born to our females had immortality, while the ones born to the humans did not. The children born to our women were kept in our compounds to conceal that fact. The talents the children exhibited became diluted when they again bred with humans, and became enhanced if they bred with our people."

That was exactly what my family's mythology had said! So I needed to trace the family that went toward what was today Western Europe. Putting the book aside after photographing as much as I could of the story, I went looking for another book just like it but for a group that left for Europe.

I had no idea how long I was there. It was many hours, possibly days. Strangely, I never got hungry or thirsty. Usually hunger lets me know what time it was. My eyes were tired, but I wasn't sleepy: another anomaly, because you'd think that if I had been awake longer than a day, I'd be dragging ass and falling asleep. Maybe it was because what I was reading was so fascinating.

I stood up and stretched my legs, back, arms, and neck. Looking around for a clock or something that would indicate time, I found nothing.

"Hey there," I called out, not really expecting an answer.

"Yes, Lora?" came the disembodied voice again. "How can I help you?"

"Um, how long have I been here?"

"You have been reading for the equivalent of 2.34 days outside."

"Two days? How come I'm not hungry or tired?"

"Because time flows differently here. It has only been a few hours."

"Oh, that's convenient," I said. "I think I should be going though. May I return to do some more research?"

"Of course, Lora, you may return as many times as you like."

"Thanks. Um, how do I get out of here?"

The answer to my question was a door appearing to my right in the middle of the floor. It had a strange glow around it.

"Please use the door to the right to exit. When you exit, it will be at the same place and time you left to come here."

Oh! That was handy! Gathering up all my materials, notes, and putting it all in my bag, I thanked the voice, and walked out into bright sunlight. I walked back to my car and went home. I wanted to call Falon once I had summarized what I learned.

Chapter 18

— Falon

Lora called me a few days before I was to return to Kansas with some really interesting information. Her research had turned up evidence that there were originally at least thirty-five groups of immortals who spread across the planet.

"They call themselves Zydeans and came from another planet to Earth 30,000 years ago. When they got here, the land masses were pretty much covered in ice, so they settled on Antarctica and built a city," said Lora.

"They can live thousands of years! Mark may be a youngster in their ranks. Rick surely is. But that means that they have children and there is a parent for Rick somewhere," said Lora.

"That's exciting, Lora," I agreed. "Now what?" I asked.

"Well, I have a long way to go before getting to the part of discovering who Rick is. Maybe I can contact my friend in the RCMP about a DNA comparison."

"Do you have a friend in the RCMP?" I asked.

"Yes, he works in the division that analyzes crime scene evidence," said Lora. "They now have a computer system that analyzes and stores DNA samples. Perhaps they can find something."

"Keep me in the loop, okay?"

"No problem," she said. "This is exciting. I cannot wait to tell Rick!"

I had to return to Kansas City the next Monday. *Darn*. But at least work would keep me busy while Mark was dealing with whatever he was dealing with. I could only hope that they wouldn't kill him. As Lora said, as long as his heartbeat was synced with mine, he was okay.

That morning, my boss dragged me into his office with an announcement.

"Falon, we are having an office party so that the whole team can meet a new potential customer from Germany and socialize together."

"Ah, do I have to attend?"

"Yes, as project manager you have to be there. The rest of the team from the client will be there. It won't be anything fancy, just a barbeque here at the hotel," said Peter. "I want you there because the customer's head office bigwigs will be here from Germany. I want them to meet you."

"All right, if I have to."

"Wear that pretty green dress," he suggested.

"The one I wore to dinner with the client?" I asked.

"Yes, that one."

He was referring to a green dress that I had with a very deep neckline. It showed a lot of cleavage. Last time I wore it was with a dinner "date" with a client, when I'd been asked to entertain him, I was pretty sure that the entertainment was supposed to have been me, but Mark saved me from that situation.

"I'm not liking this being pimped out all the time, Peter," I said. "This is the last—very last—time."

"Fine. The BBQ will keep your mind off your missing boyfriend," he quipped.

"Thanks so much. You're a gem," I answered sarcastically. "I think I'll wear something different this time, thanks."

The next Friday, everyone gathered at the hotel and the hotel put on the barbeque on their patio. It was very nice. They had a huge fireplace outside too, and tables and chairs. Away from the patio, in a secluded spot hidden by well-placed shrubbery, about fifty feet away, I found a garden swing facing a pretty fountain in a pond. *This is a perfect place to hide from the crowd. They can't see me here, and I can sit here by the pond and watch the fish swim around.* They were pretty fish—all kinds of colors.

The lead programmer spotted me going that way and followed me with two glasses in his hand.

"Hi, Falon, I thought you could use a margarita," he said, handing me one of the glasses.

"Oh, you're a lifesaver. Thank you very much," I said.

"May I join you?" he asked.

"If you don't mind, no thank you. I'm kind of in the mood to be quiet if you don't mind."

"No problem." He got up. "I'll see you later, then."

I sat there watching the sunset, when I was interrupted by my boss, and he was bringing two visitors with him. *Great, these are the dorks I had to meet.* Getting up, straightening my skirt and checking that no cleavage was showing, I stood before they got here.

"Falon, there you are. These are the gentlemen I was speaking to you about this morning. They are from the executive head office. They have another project that we will be moving to next. Falon, this is Hans and Piotre. Gentlemen, this is our project manager, Falon Robertson."

"Please to meet you, gentlemen," I said, holding out my hand to the first man.

"*Fraulein*, it is a pleasure to meet you. Peter here has told us very nice things about you." Hans smiled as he spoke. He couldn't stop himself from looking at my chest. It wasn't a glance either.

"Falon, what a treat to meet you," gushed Piotre as he took my hand. He held on to it just a bit too long for my liking. At least his glance was a glance and he focused on my face as he was speaking. Unfortunately, he was drunk. I could tell from the slight slur in his words. "May I sit with you so we can discuss the new project we want to do?"

I wanted to say no, but with my boss watching, I couldn't.

"Sure, let's have a seat and you can tell me all about it. Is the swing okay with you?" I asked.

"Delightful," Piotre replied. He sat down quickly on one end. The other two had already turned around and were walking away. *Why did I feel like I was being set up?*

The conversation started out business-like. Piotr was drinking a lot of alcohol and his speech became slurred. He went and ordered another round of drinks for both of us and handed me one. I took a sip and thought it tasted funny. So I decided not to have any more. I started getting concerned when he started watching me carefully.

"How do you feel, *fraulein*?" he asked me.

"Like I've had quite enough to drink, thank you. I should be going," I said, and tried to stand up. I couldn't. My legs didn't react. Worse yet, my head started swimming. Piotre leaned back in the swing and tipped his head back and smiled.

"You see, *fraulein*, you and I are going to have a private party, *ja*?" he said quietly. He took hold of one hand and lifted my fingers to his lips and bit them.

I was starting to panic; my body was going numb. He had drugged me. Now I couldn't really move much. I tested my other hand and it still obeyed—good.

"You are so beautiful, *fraulein*," he said quietly. "I want to eat you."

"Um, that is not going to happen. I'm sorry," I tried to pull my hand away and couldn't. He held it fast as he reached for my neck. His hand circled my throat, choking my airway.

"I think it will if I say it will." He dropped my hand and grabbed my boob outside the shirt. There was no gentleness about it. Crushing my boob in his hand, he exposed my bra.

"Take your hands off me," I growled. "I do not consent to this!" But my voice came out as a squeak, my vocal cords being compressed too much. *Oh, Goddess help me! I can't do this! Where is Mark? I need him right now!*

"Oh, my kitten growls," Hans chortled. "This is nice, *ja?*" He was pinching and squeezing my boob like it was a softball. I couldn't really do much to cause a big loud scene so that this would be discovered. I didn't want to make a scene, because it would be humiliating, but anything would be better than this.

"Either you take your hands off me now or I will hurt you," I growled, louder. But still it didn't sound like anything coherent. *Why did I come over here by myself?* I realized this was a stupid idea. *I should never have come to this bloody BBQ.*

"Help!" I tried to squeak out. "Help me!"

That only served to excite him more. He scooched closer, and while he was abusing my boob, his mouth landed on mine and crushed my lips. He tried spearing his tongue into my mouth but I wouldn't let him, keeping my teeth closed.

"Come on, *fraulein*, we can have some fun when it gets dark," he slobbered.

"Get off me!" I tried to yell. I was getting very angry. I tried again to push him away, but he was too heavy and strong.

Where is my immortal strength? I only had one arm still working.

His hand pulled my boob out of my shirt and pushed on it to get at the nipple. Opening more buttons, he had one side of me hanging out completely. He dove on my boob like it was a popsicle, biting for real and licking. The traitorous appendage responded of course. Seeing that my boob liked what he was doing, he went after the other. Freeing it from my bra cup, he pulled it out of my shirt too. Now that both were topside, he lasciviously licked both of them, going back and forth from one to the other, while not taking his hand from my neck.

My nipples decided to mutiny on me and puckered up. Moving even closer, he removed the hand from my throat and grabbed both boobs at once and smashed them together. His tongue fucked my cleavage until I was completely wet, because of course the body responds even when the brain says *stop.*

I didn't know how long I'd been sitting there immobilized, but it was getting dark. The swing I had chosen was off away from the crowd; no one really could see anything from the main party. So no help was going to intervene. I had to get this lech off me on my own. *Where is my immortal strength?*

Since my hands were free to move at the moment, I tried to break his grip by sweeping them up inside his arms. I didn't have enough force with just one hand, but it distracted him for a split second. He looked at me, and that was when I poked him in the eye with the only hand that sort of worked. He slapped me with everything he had, bringing tears to my eyes and making my face sting like it was on fire.

"You are not finished until I say so," he growled at me.

God, why is he so strong? Oh please, Goddess, help me! Mark! Please help, Mark.

He grabbed me by the throat again and lifted me off the swing cushion and dragged me over to a park bench. He pushed me down so that I stretched out. He manipulated my legs so that one was bent over the back of the bench and my skirt was around my waist. Then he forced my legs apart.

His hands started a journey up the inside of my legs to my panties. I tried to move my legs close together, but his hands were brutally strong, forcing them apart.

"Keep your legs open for me, *fraulein*," he commanded.

I grunted, shaking my head emphatically *NO! I could shake my head!*

He not so gently pulled my panties aside and thrust three fingers up my vagina and started finger fucking me. When his thumb pressed on my clit, I was prepared to experience the worst betrayal possible. But it didn't happen. Instead all my senses went numb and dry. My body shut down.

Trying to think of something I could do to stop this, I had to watch as he assaulted one part of my body then another. Strangely, I couldn't feel anything. I disassociated somehow so that it looked like someone else. I wanted to kick him in the balls and was thinking of how I could accomplish this if he tried to use his filthy little penis.

He was getting very excited by finger fucking me. He again had a hand holding me down by my throat, so strong he was almost choking me. He ripped my panties off and the three fingers continued their assault on my body.

Oh no. The final assault. Oh, Goddess, God, don't let this happen, please! Mark! I screamed in my head over and over his name.

Without taking his hand from my neck, he pulled me onto the ground. He undid his fly and a cock the size of something inhuman popped out. That was never going to fit. It didn't matter to him. He clamped my mouth shut; he looked around for something. Finding my panties, he rolled them up and shoved them in my mouth and covered it with his hand … I cringed waiting for the final assault …

"This is how the family council punishes disobedience," he murmured. He levered his cock between my legs. I felt a fist pushing into me. It was so wide I screamed under his hand. He stretched me so far that I thought I would split.

But like a siren had gone off, suddenly Mark was there! He was an astral projection, but he was there with all his glory, red eyes and fangs completely on display.

"Get off her now or you die," growled Mark.

My attacker looked up from where he was and saw the visage of Mark as a demon. I could see him blink as if he didn't believe his eyes.

"You!" screamed Mark.

My assailant turned around and faced me again.

Mark reached for him with a hand that had very sharp claws on it and grabbed his shoulder.

"I said get off now! I won't repeat myself," he said with menace. As soon as his hand made contact, my attacker turned around again screamed in terror when he realized the huge monster standing behind him with glowing red eyes was real. Still, he didn't move off me.

Mark somehow solidified before my eyes and pulled him off me, with one hand flinging him into the tree beside me. He followed him and attacked without any hesitation. I curled up into a tight ball and passed out.

When I came to, Mark was holding me in his arms and rocking me.

"Oh my poor beautiful girl. I'm so sorry I couldn't be here faster."

I couldn't speak and I couldn't move myself. I couldn't move. Everything hurt.

Mark tried to straighten my clothes so I would be covered. I was bleeding from the assault in several places.

"He's drugged you," said Mark. "Your body should clear that in half an hour and then you'll be able to speak and move. I will stay here until you are able to do that."

Mark's here?

"I'm not physically here, love. I'm a projection, similar to the time when you were being stalked. This time though, so much power came through your fear that it made me solid too, even though I am still in that cell. I don't know how long this will last."

He's not here, but I see him. He's holding me.

He continued holding and rocking me until the lights around the patio started coming on. That meant it must be around 8:30 p.m. I tried to speak. Nothing came out yet. I tried to swallow and the muscles in my throat strained to move. My mouth was so dry.

"You're trying to swallow?" asked Mark. "Just a second." He got up after placing me on the ground and went to find something. He returned with a few ice cubes in his hand.

"Here, suck on this for a minute," he said, placing the piece of ice in my mouth. That was better. Much needed liquid lubricated my tongue and throat, making it easier to make a sound.

"Not here?" I managed to croak out.

"No, not really."

"Disappear again?"

"Yes, I think so," he said. "But you're safe now. He won't be attacking you again."

I managed to turn my head and look over at the tree and saw a bloody object on the ground. *How was I going to explain that? How was I going to explain being raped and then a demon saving me?*

"Dead?" I asked in another croak.

"No, he's not dead, just injured. It looks worse than it is. It looks like an animal attack."

Mark stayed with me for a while, at least until the shaking finally stopped and I could sit up gingerly.

I watched him as he seemed to become transparent, and then turn to wisps of smoke as he vanished in the darkness. I looked around me now that I could move. My attacker had pulled me into a secluded area behind the swing to finish his deed. Thankfully, Mark had salvaged most of my clothes so my boobs were not hanging out. And I found my phone. That was an accomplishment in the dark.

I stood up cautiously because my legs were still unstable. What should I do? Do I call the police? *How do I report this?* How do I report that someone started raping me but my boyfriend showed up and stopped it? *Oh, but he's not here, he's imprisoned in a cell somewhere.* I didn't want to have to explain this to everyone. Mark had said it would look like an animal attack. But from where? *Do I go to the police station?* They'll look at me and think I've lost my mind. I looked around the patio area and saw that there was no one else around outside. The BBQ had shut down; the only lights were low, dim garden lights lighting the paths. *Do I risk running for my room?* There was a double set of doors across the patio from me. I felt so embarrassed; I didn't want anyone to find me, which was stupid because there was nothing to be embarrassed about, except the state of dress I was in. I didn't have any friends in this city yet, not like in Georgia, when I could have counted on Charity for help.

I spotted a sign pointing to restrooms accessible from the patio. I sort of ran over to the ladies' room. My legs were still unsteady. I slumped down the wall and sat on the floor. I decided to call Lora.

She answered the phone. "Falon, what's up, girl?"

"Lora, help, I've just been attacked."

"No fucking way!"

"Unfortunately, yes. At least Mark saved me. I don't know what to do," I said quietly. "I hurt so much." I was crying again. The tears were silently falling down my face this time. Unbidden, the heaves started as my body started going into shock. Racking sobs escaped my mouth as I struggled to control myself.

Lora waited for me to get it out. "Okay, start from the beginning for me."

I related what I could to her about what had happened. Including the state that Mark left my attacker in.

"Hon, you have to go to the police," Lora said gently.

"I don't know if I can," I sobbed.

"Why ever not?"

"Because no one will believe this happened," I sobbed some more.

"Then we'll make them believe. That creep will get away with it if you don't report it," she said.

"He was not an American—he is visiting, and he's a prospective client of the company!" I screamed. "How am I going to cope with this?"

The sobs came on strong again. My body was having difficulty catching a breath because I was crying so hard. The pain was double, physical and emotional.

"Falon! Listen to me, girl, listen," came Lora's voice. She managed to break through the noise in my head. "Falon, can you get up to your room—or, oh my God, did it happen in your room?"

"No, it didn't happen in the room."

"Good, so can you get to your room?" she asked.

"I don't know if I can do it without being seen. My clothes are a mess. There are grass stains all over them, and the top is ripped, and I think I am bleeding too."

"So you look like you've been nearly raped?" she asked.

"I guess so," I chuckled. That helped. "I'm a mess."

"Well, God forbid that you be raped neatly! You're alive though, so thanks for that," she confessed.

"Thanks to Mark."

"Yeah, we have to figure that one out," said Lora. "Okay, you've got this, girl. You can make it upstairs. I'll stay with you on the phone. Is there any way you can tell them you fought him off?"

"Lora, I couldn't fight him."

"That isn't surprising. Our strength often disappears when we're assaulted."

"No, my immortal strength wasn't there. I couldn't fight him."

"Hmm, I'll look into that. Did he drug you?"

"Yes, I noticed my limbs getting really weak before anything started. I thought I was drinking too much."

"You don't get drunk, Falon, remember?"

"Mark said it would take half an hour for my body to clean the drug from my system. He was right."

"So, you couldn't have fought him off. We have to think of something else. We can just leave it at something pulled him off you and left him a bloody pulp under a tree."

"I know. I can't say anything that will draw attention to the family or my species."

I pulled myself up off the floor and got some paper towels and washed my face a bit. Taking a look at myself in the mirror, I wasn't as messy as I was afraid. But there were stains on my dress and bloodstains on the back. *Hopefully, no one will notice.* The bathroom had an exit out into the hotel lobby too, so I went that way instead of across the patio.

When I opened the bathroom door, I was relieved to see that I was in a hallway off to one side of the lobby, one of the elevator hallways.

"Okay, the way is clear, so I'm going to my room. Will you stay on the phone with me?"

"Of course."

I quickly walked to the elevators and pushed the up button. A car came right away, and I was able to get on by myself. So far so good.

Pressing the top floor, I was relieved it had no stops.

Getting out, I looked both ways, and the hall was empty.

"I'm on my floor. The hallway is empty." With my phone to my ear, talking to Lora, I walked down the hallway to my room and let myself inside. As soon as I closed the door, my body shattered. I let out a quiet scream.

"Falon, are you okay?" Lora asked. "Of course you're not okay, but are you in one piece?"

"Hon?" she said.

"Hon, are you there?" she repeated

"Falon!" Lora yelled.

"Yes, I'm here. I'm in one piece. No one's here but me and the door is locked," I answered.

"Good, go have a hot shower and call me back when you're in bed. Okay?"

"Okay."

A hot shower was a good idea. I needed to wash that filth off my body, and I wanted to give myself a douche to clean myself inside. But I couldn't if I was calling the police. I just let the water course over me. It felt like his hands were still on my throat and belly, holding me down. I paid particular attention to washing my poor breasts, which were scratched and bruised from the mishandling. Thank goodness for hotel water pressure. That hot shower lasted forty-five minutes. Getting out, I grabbed the hotel's fluffy bathrobe and wrapped myself in it.

Climbing into bed, I called Lora back.

"How are you doing?" was the first question out of her mouth.

"I'm doing better. Thanks for being there," I said.

"Anytime. I wish I could be there in person," she said.

"Me too," I answered. "What do I do? If I go to the police, they won't believe me or do anything because we're both visitors to this country."

"Maybe, or maybe not," she said. "You don't know unless you try. Let's figure out a story that will make sense and not give away Mark's participation."

"What about telling them I passed out and don't know what happened?"

"That might work."

"I'll call the station and ask if I can file a report."

"Let me know what happens. And order dinner for yourself. You need to eat to regain normalcy. You need to do normal things."

"Okay. I will."

"Bye, love."

"Bye."

Chapter 19

— Falon

I first ordered some food from the kitchen. Comfort food—a grilled cheese sandwich and tomato soup. And then I took a deep breath and called the police.

"Station 57, how can we help you?"

"Hello, Officer. I have a hypothetical question. If a foreigner assaults another foreigner, should the victim report the crime here if the crime happened here?" I asked.

"That's a tricky one, Miss. What sort of crime was it? Hypothetically speaking, of course."

"Rape, or attempted rape."

"Oh my. And neither victim nor perp are US citizens?"

"That is correct. Neither is a US citizen."

"I'd have to speak to my superior officer to get you an answer. Do you mind waiting a minute?"

"No, not at all."

A few minutes later there was a knock on my door.

"Who is it?"

"Room service, ma'am."

"Can you come in? I'm on the phone with the police."

"Yes, ma'am," The door opened and the bellhop brought in a tray with my dinner on it.

"I left ten dollars on the table there for you. Thank you."

"Thank you, ma'am."

A few seconds later, the cop was back on the line.

"Miss?"

"Yes, I'm here, Officer."

"It seems that would be a very complex case. We could open a file, but unfortunately, it would depend on who their home countries were as to if we could actually get justice for the victim."

"That's what I was afraid of."

"Miss, is this hypothetical victim yourself?"

"Yes, it is," I admitted, as the tears started flowing again.

"Miss, are you alright? Can I send an officer over to check on you?"

"I'm staying in a hotel. It would cause a real ruckus to have the police show up."

"Miss, I don't rightly care what it looks like," said the officer. "If you've been raped, you may need medical attention. At the very least, can I have a lady officer come and do a rape kit? We may not be able to get you justice, but we sure as hell can prevent that filth from returning to the country."

"Don't I have to go to the hospital for that?" I asked.

"No, Miss, we can have a nurse and lady officer take the evidence in your residence—or hotel room in this case—to protect your privacy as much as possible. This is important, because this will hopefully give us his DNA."

"But I have showered—I had to—to get the smell of him off of me. I have probably washed all the evidence away."

"Do you know your attacker?"

"He was introduced to me by my boss at the hotel."

"So you have his name?"

"Yes, I know his name. He was introduced to me right before at a company BBQ."

"That's very good, Miss. Along with whatever other physical evidence the nurse can gather, it will help us build a profile. Rapists are habitual creatures. They don't do it just once. If we can build a case, we can stop him."

"All right. Send an officer for the rape kit. I'm staying at the Holiday Inn, room 407."

"They'll be there in thirty minutes. They won't use sirens, and they'll be plainclothes. No ruckus. I promise."

"Thank you."

After hanging up the phone, I went and took my tray to sit on the couch and watch television. It was good to eat something not fancy. The knock on the door came thirty minutes later as promised. Looking through the peephole, I saw two women. One showed me her badge.

"Thank you for letting us in. I am Officer Shandie and this is Nurse Whiltshire. Why don't I ask you the questions while the nurse is doing the kit."

"All right," I said. "I've already taken a shower."

"Don't worry about that, there will still be plenty of evidence," said the nurse.

It was a humiliating experience. What I hadn't realized was that since it had been an hour or more since the incident, the bruising was starting to show. They needed me to strip completely so that they could photograph every part of me. They took skin samples, scraped under my nails, took swabs inside and out.

Nothing was overlooked. There must have been fifty little packages sealed up and put in the kit bag. All the while, the officer carefully questioned me about what happened, how I felt, where it happened. I felt like I was under interrogation. She assured me it was to make sure they had a complete picture, as complete as possible.

The nurse retrieved my clothes and underwear from the garbage. They took all my clothes as evidence because there was a possibility that a trace was left behind. The officer sent another police officer to retrieve the panties and napkins I had thrown in the trash bin and look for the bra.

After they had asked all their questions, they got me to sign the witness statement and give them my contact information.

It took me a while to calm down and collect myself again. Speaking to Lora helped. She had a way of cutting through the crap in my head and getting down to the essence of me. She made me promise to take something to help me sleep.

After I got off the phone, I went and had another shower to attempt to wash away the feeling of being exposed and dirty, and crawled into bed with a cup of tea and a good book. It wasn't long before my eyelids were so heavy I couldn't keep them open anymore. Closing my book, I snuggled into the soft pillows and comforter. I left the lights on though. I didn't want the darkness right now.

Mark came to me in my dreams.

I was walking down a straight, smooth path. There was a bench up ahead and I decided to sit on it. A slight touch on my shoulder made me turn around and I was looking into Mark's eyes. He was not solid. *I can see through him.* He raised a hand and caressed my cheek.

"Oh, my poor love," he crooned. "I'm so sorry I'm not there for you right now."

"Mark, I really need you now. I don't know how to keep it together."

"You can, my love. You're stronger than you think. I will be free again soon and be reunited with you," he reassured me.

"Thank you for saving me," I said to him.

"I only wish I could have been there sooner."

His hand caressed my cheek, brushing the hair back from my face. He leaned in and placed the most soft, sensual kiss on my lips. His astral form comforted me and held me close. Even though he wasn't there, I felt safe in his arms.

"Let me give you pleasure, to heal," Mark said gently.

"No, just hold me, please."

Mark laid his hands on me and infused me with his energy. I felt endorphins spreading through my body, then a sense of calm flowed over me like a gentle wave.

He kissed me again, tenderly.

"You'll be alright now," he whispered in my ear.

"Don't go!" I begged him.

"I'll be with you soon. I'm only a thought away," he crooned. He was getting thinner now, more transparent as his projection left.

The feeling of contentment and happiness had relaxed me, and I fell deeper into the dream and sleep. Mark would be back soon.

I woke up the next morning realizing that I'd dreamt of Mark last night, that he had visited me again, to give me comfort. Then I remembered his promise: he would return soon. He was coming back.

He came to me to replace the ugliness of the rape with the love of his body. Again, he was healing me. I'm not sure it would have worked as well if he'd been here in person. I don't know if I could have let anyone touch me after yesterday. But what he did for me in my dream showed me I could recover.

Outside the bedroom, a door opened and closed with a click. Someone was in my room! I opened my eyes a second to confirm that the bedroom door was closed. I heard a quiet knock on the door and someone said, "Housekeeping."

Oh geez, the maid.

"I'm still in bed," I called out.

"Okay, Miss, I'll just clean up this room for you and leave the bedroom 'til you have left," said the maid.

Oh crap.

"Are you okay, Miss?" came a quiet voice.

"Yes, I'm fine," I responded.

Finally, I heard the door open and close again. I got up and went to the bathroom. Glancing in the mirror, I could still see the bruises around my throat, on my breasts, and pelvis where my attacker's hands had been rough.

I hugged myself. Telling myself that it was Mark's arms. *He'll be home soon. He said so.*

Chapter 20

— Mark

My eyes snapped open from the middle of my dream. Falon was in trouble! I felt her fear like it was my own. She was trying to keep it under control, but I felt her panic rising.

What is happening? What is Falon going through to scare her so much?

I felt helpless sitting there in the dark. I tried to reach out to find her. Something was blocking me. The barriers around the cell had me locked down completely. All I could do was live through the pain and fear with her. *Her heart is breaking and she feels paralysed and I can't do a fucking thing!*

Standing up, I started pacing around the cell. The energy that came off me was bouncing off the walls and amplifying everything I felt. I screamed at the top of my lungs. I started pounding on the rock walls.

My woman, my mate, my love, is in terrible pain and terrified.

And I wasn't there to save her. *I have to get out of here!*

The rage fueled my power. I didn't realize that I was charging up. My eyes were glowing and my fangs had completely extended as I yelled and beat the hell out of the walls. Somehow, I had to escape. I had to get to her to help.

I could feel the power of the emotion coming from her, and I let it wrap around me, through me, and added it to my rage. The most remarkable thing happened: I was suddenly there in front of her. When my eyes registered what was happening, my fangs punched out like the weapons they were, and my eyes glowed a deep red, allowing me to see at night clearly.

"Get off her now or you die," I growled

The attacker looked at me over his shoulder but didn't see me—or didn't believe what he was seeing and went back to what he was doing. I lost it at that moment.

I recognize you!

"You!" I screamed at him. He was an enforcer for the Council. *The council had sent him!* I *will* get to the bottom of this!

I reached for him but my hands were not solid. They had become claws, not unlike a bear's, but I couldn't grab him or do anything.

I gave him one last warning, and when he reacted I stared at my hand and willed it to be solid so I could grab his shoulder. He turned around again at the moment I felt my body solidify and screamed, but it was too late. I ripped him off Falon and threw him against a tree behind her.

Jumping on the creep, I wanted to tear him limb from limb. As it was, he had a huge claw mark gouged down his shoulder, and another on his torso as lifelong mementos. I had stopped myself because I couldn't afford to kill this human. If I did, there would be an inquiry and too much truth might come out.

Calming down took effort. Once I had regained full self-control, I looked behind me and noticed that Falon had curled up and passed out. She was out of danger but still hurt, terribly hurt. At least her heart was beating normally again.

I left the attacker slumped beside the tree as is. The police could believe whatever they wanted.

I sat on the ground and scooped Falon into my arms, holding and rocking her. I would wait until the drug wore off before leaving her alone.

I hadn't known that I could do this. It was the first time that I had managed to materialize and solidify from a projection. I think somehow it had to do with the amount of energy Falon had been putting out too. Combined, we were stronger.

She came to, and I stayed with her until she stopped shaking. By then, I could feel the solidity dissolving—I was leaving her. Drained, I passed out in my cell only to wake up hours later feeling like I'd been through hell and back. My last thought was that I had to investigate this new ability.

Chapter 21

— Lora

My best friend was nearly raped! What could I do? *Nothing!* I was stuck here in Montreal. Perhaps I could work more on getting Mark located, and on Rick's history. If I could prove they were family, maybe Rick could help.

After I talked with Falon last month I was so jazzed to find more out about the Olde Ones. *Has it only been a couple of weeks since then?*

I needed to reach out to my friend in the RCMP and see if they could run DNA tests that would show connections or similarities between the four of us.

It had been about a year since I had spoken to them, so I hoped they were still in that position.

"Hello there, I'm looking for Jeff Larson?" I asked when I got the receptionist.

"One moment please," she answered. "Yes, Jeff is at extension 352. I will transfer you now."

A few seconds later, a very deep voice answered the phone. I remembered that voice. It used to send shivers down my back. When I learned Jeff was non-binary, we became fast friends as he taught me what it meant and how to address non-binary people.

"Larson speaking. How can I help?" they said.

"Hello, Jeff, it's Lora. How are you doing?" I asked.

"Lora O'Reilly? Wow, not someone I expected to hear from. I'm fine, you?"

"I'm doing great, thanks. I'm calling to pick your brains about DNA."

"Oh, okay. Shoot."

"If I get four samples from different people who may have a familial connection, can we find it with DNA? Or if they have similar characteristics, can we see that in DNA?"

"Well, we can certainly determine family connections, and how far apart they are generationally. We can see if they have traits in common, but not perhaps what the traits are. We can also determine what is in common between species. We all share a lot of DNA—between plants and animals and humans."

"That's fascinating. How long would it take, and where would I go to get it done?" I asked.

"A few weeks for a full analysis, and you'd need to find a private lab who does this sort of work. It's more complex than determining paternity."

"Would it be expensive, do you think?" I asked.

"A few hundred dollars, I would expect," they answered. "Who is this for? If you don't mind me asking."

"A friend of mine was adopted and he's trying to find his birth family. Interestingly enough, he has some very specific characteristics that he shares with another friend of mine, so we're wondering if they are in the same family."

"You mean like a mutation that is rare?"

"Yeah, sort of like that. Something that is very unique anyway."

"Sounds interesting. Perhaps I can run some of the DNA here at the lab. We have the best equipment after all,"

"I need to keep it very confidential—like I mean it cannot go anywhere, not to the RCMP, the police, anyone. Is that possible?"

"Hmm, now I'm even more intrigued. Yes, I can keep it a secret."

"Okay, I'll work on getting samples. Three of the people are out of town right now, but you can start with me," I said.

"You? Are you one of the 'possible common characteristics' people?"

"Yes, there may be a common link between the four of us, but it would be ancient. Like back dozens of generations," I explained.

"Well, let me draw some blood today. Come to my lab after work, say around 5:30 today? I'll meet you at the front door security to let you in."

"Okay, that would be great. Will you get into trouble?"

"Only if I get caught," they said, chuckling.

At 5:30, I was waiting at the front door security desk. They had called Jeff and they were on their way.

"Lora!" I heard Jeff call across the lobby. "Wow, you still look amazing. Look at you. Oh my! You're happy!"

"Well, yes I am, thanks. How did you know?"

"You're glowing. A new fella??"

"Now, why does it have to be a guy to make me happy?"

"Oh, I dunno," they said slyly.

"Yes, it is a new guy," I admitted. "He's very special. He's a chef in Atlanta."

"How did you meet him?"

"On a trip down south to meet my best friend, Falon. She ended up making a foursome and Rick was my blind date."

"Very cool. I love to hear stories like that. It means magic still exists, and finding love is really a matter of luck, or fate," said Jeff.

"I remember, you're a strong believer in fate," I said. "As a scientist, how does that work?"

"Fate puts things together, science makes it work," Jeff said simply. "Let's go, eh?"

I followed Jeff down to their lab, which was underground. Apparently, they put it there to protect it from some kinds of attacks. It was a cool-looking place. They gave me a short tour. There were huge centrifuges and electron microscopes, and other things I couldn't recognize. They sat me down to draw the blood and took a few vials.

"Do you need that much blood? Do you need a cheek swab too?" I asked.

"Not really, but some of the tests require blood, and I don't know how much usually. Buccal swabs are just different. We use similar equipment to what say *Ancestry* or *23andMe* would. Don't worry, I'm not going to put it in the RCMP database. Whatever I don't use, I'll destroy. I promise," Jeff assured me.

"Okay, please let me know what you can find out with just my DNA. I'm curious."

I left the building and got to my car. I had a funny feeling in the pit of my stomach that I couldn't identify. My phone rang.

"Hello?"

"Hello, beautiful lady," said Rick.

"Oh, Rick, it's nice to hear your voice!" I said excitedly. "Where are you?"

"I'm in Atlanta, but it's my day off, so I thought I would call you and see what you were up to. It's been a couple of weeks and I miss you terribly."

"I've got lots of information for you. I've been researching and I've found out lots of cool things. Plus, I've just spoken to a friend of mine at the RCMP and he is going to do some DNA analysis for me on my blood, and then when I get a sample from the three of you, we'll add that and see what we can learn," I said in a rush.

"Whoa! DNA tests?"

"Just to find out if you and Mark have a familial connection," I said. "Don't worry, they will keep it confidential."

"Hmm, okay. I trust you," he said. "I'm so used to hiding that letting someone see that much scares me. What if there is something alien in my blood and he … they want to lock me up?"

"I don't think that's going to happen," I said. "But if it makes you feel better, I won't be providing any names or any identifying information."

"That's good. I agree," he said.

"So what did you call for?" I asked.

"Well, what about finding time to get together this month?" he asked.

"That would be amazing. Maybe you could help me with the research. I've found a marvelous source with lots of books. It will just take a long time to go through them all."

"I would love to," said Rick. "I am very eager to find out more."

"Well, I'll tell you what I've found out so far," I said.

As I continued walking to my car, I gave him all the news about what I had found in the ancient books. Rick was making *ooo* and *ahh* sounds as I told him the details. When I gave him the time periods, he was silent for a minute. I told him I had taken notes, and that I would send him copies.

We decided on the following weekend for him to come to Montreal. He called me later that night after my kids were in bed, and we had fun on the phone again.

I missed him so much.

Chapter 22

— Falon

It was a good thing the barbeque was on a Friday night. It gave me two days to collect myself before having to be back at work. I wasn't going to let what happened to me stop me, and I sure as hell wasn't going to let anyone know.

My body healed very quickly. It was a good thing the police came right away, because by the following morning all the bruises were gone and the tears in my skin were healed. This immortality thing was handy, except when it disappeared and you needed it to stay. I just wished I had been able to fight him off.

Walking into the office that morning, I was confident that no one would suspect I had been traumatized. I held my head up high and walked with a straight back. I had put on my power suit to give myself armor. I even paid particular attention to my makeup this morning.

I didn't know if my boss was still in town or not. I hadn't seen him since he introduced those creeps. I took the elevator up to the office floor and made my way to the office designated for Peter when he was in town. Mine was next door so I dropped my briefcase off there first.

Peter's door was closed. I knocked and waited for a response.

"Come in," came Peter's voice.

"Peter," I said as I opened the door and walked in. I stopped cold when I saw those Germans still there.

"Excuse me, gentlemen, I need to speak with Falon for a minute. I'll be right back. Please help yourself to coffee and croissants on the desk there," said Peter.

He stood up and followed me out of his office.

"Let's go to your office, Falon," he said. When the door closed, he turned to me with an anxious look on his face.

"Are you alright?" he asked.

"No. And yes," I said.

"What happened? Tell me everything please," he beseeched me.

"I don't know if I want to tell you everything," I responded honestly. I took a deep breath. "Sit down, this will take a few minutes."

"What happened?"

I took another deep breath, straightened my shoulders, and began.

"Piotr attacked me on Friday. He drugged me, held me captive, and tried to rape me. He almost succeeded, but some kind person stopped it by pulling him off me. I called the police on Friday night and filed a report."

At the word *rape*, Peter sucked in his breath and his face became drawn tightly.

****

"I was afraid something had happened," he said quietly.

"Why?"

"It was the way he was boasting this morning. Something was wrong. I got the feeling of something being very, very wrong. It was visceral. What did the police say?"

"Well, the fact that I'm a Canadian and he's German means they can't do much. However, they did a full rape kit and they said they will run the DNA, and they can at least put out warnings or something. It's possible Germany would extradite him for the police to arrest. I would need to return to press charges."

"You're going to press charges, right?" he asked.

"Oh, most definitely, yes."

"Good," he said, relieved. "I'm going to cancel the sale, and I'm going to report this to the CEO of their company as well."

"Are you sure?"

"Absolutely. Even if it weren't rape, I would never do business with someone who did that to an employee of mine. That creep in Atlanta was canceled too," he said unequivocally.

"Oh, I didn't know that," I said, surprised. I didn't realize Peter knew what happened there.

"Mark Chisholm let me know of the inappropriate behavior you were subjected to at the restaurant. I apologize for that, Falon. I just don't know what is wrong with these people!"

"You've got to stop trying to pimp me out," I said, angrily. "I'm not your call girl to entertain the clients. You can start taking them out for dinner and drinks yourself. I appreciate your support, but this was the last time. Now, I need to get to work."

I really didn't want to dwell on this anymore.

"Of course. Falon, we have a trauma doctor, if you need someone to speak to. And I want you to take some time off. I have some ass to kick," stated Peter. He left my office with a grim expression on his face.

I overheard Peter yelling at the two Germans and then calling the police. I stood at my window. I had a view of the elevator. It was nice to watch their sorry asses being escorted by security down the elevator and out to the parking lot. They delivered them both to the police waiting outside. The police basically dragged them by the biceps until they were off the sidewalk and tossed them into the back of a black SUV. One of them fell over his feet, landing hard on his back on the pavement. The police, not too gently, picked him up and tossed him into the vehicle. *Good riddance!*

I called Lora after dinner. I let her know that there was a police investigation and that the RCMP and Interpol had been notified. I described how they were manhandled out the door and given the bum's rush to the parking lot. Lora laughed her ass off at the description I gave her. That made me feel better. Now all that was left to do was to get on with life, because while my life had been temporarily trashed, I couldn't let that have an impact on the rest of my world.

Chapter 23

— Lora

I told Falon that Rick was coming up to Montreal next weekend to help with some of the research. I made contact with Jeff at the RCMP, and they said they'd start doing a work-up on my blood first. I mentioned that I wasn't going to give the RCMP tech anyone's real names, except mine of course.

I was waiting for Rick at the airport and waved my arms like a crazy woman as soon as I saw him come through the arrivals doorway. Running up to him, as soon as he saw me running he dropped his bags at his side and caught me with both arms. I flung my arms around his neck and laid a big kiss on him, my feet dangling off the floor.

"Wow, that's a nice welcome home!" Rick said into my ear as he hugged me hard. When he wrapped himself around my small and huggable frame, it felt like coming home.

"I missed you!" I said. "Three weeks is an eternity without you."

"I'm here now, so let's get out of this crowd and have some one-on-one time," suggested Rick.

"Follow me. I'm parked in the temporary lot," I said.

On the way home, I explained how the two occult stores worked, and mentioned that one of them was in another dimension. Only supernatural people were allowed inside, so he would be good to accompany me.

Once we got home, Rick said he wouldn't do any book shopping until he had thoroughly pleasured me, so our first stop was upstairs in the bedroom.

Rick sat on the bed while I did a striptease for him. When I got down to my skinny jeans and slipped them down over my hips, he stood up, walked to me, reached around my back to grab my ass, and lifted me up to kiss me deeply.

"I can't wait, I'm too impatient," he said.

I finished sliding out of my skinny jeans, and when Rick saw I wasn't wearing underwear, he sucked in his breath in anticipation. I had also prepared a little surprise for him. I'd shaved my pussy so that it was naked and smooth.

Of course, I bent over to discard the skinny jeans and red stilettos. That exposed my slit to him in its entirety.

Rick knelt on the floor behind me and buried his face in my slit. He could smell my arousal, and licked up the sweet juices I was secreting. When he discovered my naked pussy, he just about squealed in delight.

"Um, could you put your shoes back on, please," he requested. "They make you so fucking sexy and hot, I want to make love to you with them on."

"All right," I said, slipping my feet into them.

He picked me up, laid me on the bed, and pulled me to its edge. Spreading my legs wide, he dove between them. Starting with my clit, he pushed his tongue between my folds, and scooped up the wetness that had dripped there from before. Taking my clit between his lips, he nipped and sucked on it alternatively. I started groaning and calling out as my arousal went through the ceiling.

Then he speared his tongue and plunged into my vagina. Pushing in as far as possible, he flicked it quickly back and forth. I got even more wet and he sucked up my juices and licked his lips. He licked me from back to clit. I wiggled and arched my back as the sensations drove me crazy.

"Play with my ass," I suggested.

Rick inserted a finger into my ass, and two into my vagina, while he played with my clit in his mouth. Applying pressure with his fingers going in and out together, my panting and keening got louder as I felt my climax coming on very fast.

He brought me to the very edge and stopped. Then he slipped another finger into my ass. I spread my legs farther to open myself completely. Taking my own hands, I added them to Rick's, inserting a finger in with his two. The tightness was delightful.

"I want you inside me," I said. "The back door."

"I've not done that before," he answered.

"Use lots of lube. It's over there on the dresser."

Rick continued to stimulate me with his fingers while he took his cock out and jeans off. Standing behind me, he pulled the lube from my dresser and got himself really lubed up. I removed my fingers, cleaning them on wipes.

As he pushed against me, I could feel the pressure of his size. He was a large man, and I was very tight. He took some more lube and slathered up my ass inside and out. He again tried to slowly push his cock into me. The sweet pressure pushed me over the edge and I climaxed with a scream of delight.

"Are you okay?" he asked, worried.

"Ah, yeah, just peachy," I said. "How far in are you?"

"Not far, barely my head," he said. "How are you doing?"

"It hurts, but it's a sweet pain. Push again."

Rick added more lube to his cock and my ass, and pushed himself in some more.

"Oh, my God. Ah, oh shit!"

"Too much?" he asked.

"No. I'm not sure. Wait a sec."

"Okay, give me more," I said after a moment.

He pushed again, and I could feel my body give slightly, making room for his cock. It was like he had made it past the gate, and now it wasn't as tight.

"Ahhh, that is good. It's not as tight a feeling. How much is inside?" I asked again.

"About eight inches."

"Give me more," I said. He pushed into me until I felt his balls brush against my body.

"That's it, that's all of me," he said. "How do you feel?"

"Great, this feels great. Please continue."

"I'm entirely inside now," he said. "This adds a different sensation than I've felt before."

"Do you like it?" I asked.

As he pulled out slowly and pushed in again, he added more lube to keep us wet.

"Mmm ah, oh, yeah, go, go, mmm hmm," came out of my mouth as Rick slowly fucked me.

"Most definitely, this is exquisite," he said.

He reached around the front of me and played with my clit too while he was moving. That ramped up my arousal to a nine out of ten. I couldn't hold myself back as I took control of the motion and started using more force on him, pushing him into me harder and faster.

"Lora, this is going to finish me," he warned.

"Come, then. Ride this with me."

So he added his own urgency to mine and started to move faster, while still making sure he went as deep as he could.

"Ah, ah, ah, oh my. Oh my. OH MY!" he screamed as he pushed deep into me and released.

I could feel his seed filling me up, and it was a very different sensation.

Rick bent over me, spent—but I wasn't. For some reason, that had energized me.

"Now I want to make love with you," I said, as Rick pulled out.

"So do I," he said.

I turned around and grasped his cock, which was still very much hard and ready to go. "I see he's not finished."

"He's never finished," Rick said. "Especially around you."

Pulling open the drawer next to my bed, I grabbed a new package of sanitizing wet towels. I took out one of the wet wipes and started to clean off his cock. I pulled down the foreskin and made sure I got every inch of him. It started to excite him even more. Now he had a clean and very hard cock. This time, after I turned around, he lifted my bottom so that I lined up perfectly with his now very eager member.

As he slipped inside me, he made a comparison between how tight my ass was and how perfect a fit my vagina was.

"I still prefer this way," he decided.

Bending over the bed, he could really push further inside. I wiggled my bottom to encourage him. He was touching my cervix inside. I cooed, and my hips started moving again. As he filled me up, I squeezed him and held him in a long hug. I pressed back against him, nudging him against my cervix again.

"Oh," I moaned. "That is my favorite erogenous zone."

"Really? I can feel I'm at the end of your channel."

"Yes, there is a spot near the entrance to the womb. Some call it the A-spot. With the right man, it provides the most explosive orgasm ever," I explained.

"I'm there. I can feel the end of your vagina. Now what do you want me to do?" he asked.

"This works best if I'm sitting on you, and you're on your back," I said.

Rick pulled out and stretched out on the bed on his back. His cock was standing straight up.

I turned around and smiled when I saw his cock. Before getting up, I couldn't help grasping him with my hands and giving him a little mouth action. His cock throbbed in my hand as I wrapped my soft lips around his head. After restimulating it, I got up and straddled him. Positioning his cock right under my vagina, I sank down on his shaft until there was nothing left. He was completely inside me; his head was butting up against the end of my channel. It was the most exquisite pain ever.

I started moving in circles, grinding myself on his groin. Rick touched different parts of my channel inside, front and back, as he slid in and out.

I was quickly losing control, my orgasm building again. The pressure on his head increased as he again expanded. We came together in an explosion. I climaxed, and he for sure felt me ejaculate too—he erupted inside me, adding his semen to my juices.

His fangs were completely elongated; his gums looked aching for him to bite down. I offered him my neck.

As he sank his fangs into my shoulder, the aphrodisiac hit my bloodstream and gave me another orgasm. We shared the euphoria as we rode the orgasms together.

It took a while for us both to come down from the high. When we did, I was flaked out on top of him and completely limp.

Rick wrapped his arms around me and whispered into my ear.

"I am completely and irrevocably in love with you. I would do anything to protect and to keep you."

I stirred, and my eyes fluttered open. I moved my head to balance on my chin, looking into his eyes as he was looking at me.

"Hello, lover," I said seductively. "That was some ride."

"That it was," he said. "You know, I have never done that before."

"What, backdoor fucking?" I asked.

"Yeah, that," he said, blushing slightly.

"Oh, Rick, you were an anal novice?" I was teasing him. "How did you like it?"

"I was afraid to hurt you, frankly," he said. "I would have thought I was too big for that opening, shall we say."

"You were a little," I admitted. "But my body adapted, and after it was amazing, especially if I have something in my vagina too. I cannot explain the sensations. It's like being taken twice."

"Is that a fantasy of yours? To have two men at the same time?" he asked, not looking like he really wanted the answer.

"I don't know if it's possible," I said. "Is there room for two guys that way?" I was blushing a little.

"Do we want to go there?" he asked quietly. "I'm not sure I want to share you with another man, even if I want to pleasure you in whatever way you need."

"You're such a sweet man," I said. "It is a fantasy of mine. But it's not one I have to do with two men. Toys work just fine. Next time you can play with one of them if you want."

"I would try anything with you," he said with a thick voice. "After all, who am I to deny you pleasure?"

"Hmm, I'll try to think up something interesting for us to try, then," I said coquettishly.

We lay there in each other's arms in complete contentment. Rick dozed off, and I was catnapping while concocting a game for us to play.

Waking up refreshed a few hours later, I was ready to go to the occult store again.

Rick was still spooning me, his arms holding me in an embrace. I rolled over onto my back and kissed his nose.

"Hello, beautiful," he murmured to me. "I cannot get over how much I love holding you while you sleep. I ... I'm completely addicted to you."

"Hello, handsome," I responded. "I feel the same, and at the risk of jumping the gun, I could fall for you really hard—if I haven't already, that is."

"I ... I'm already in love with you. I want to make a life with you somehow. My dreams are all about how I am going to do this," he said. "If I am immortal as you think, I don't know how we can make it work."

"If you are the immortal I think you are, we may have an avenue open to us," I said. "But we need to learn more about yours and Mark's species. Which is why I want to go to the occult store again with you."

"Well, let's get dressed and get going," he said. "Can we grab something to eat on the way?"

"That's a good idea," I said. "Time flows differently there, and we'll be hungry—well, I'm starving now after all that remarkable sex."

Chuckling, Rick sat up and pulled me up with him. Holding on to me for just a moment, he kissed me tenderly with his luscious lips, and then smacked my bottom as he stood up.

"Oh, don't start that," I said with a grin. "Or I'll pull you down on the bed again and have you spank me more!"

Rick glanced at me and smiled knowingly. He understood dominance and could play that game very successfully. I would be a scrappy submissive, and he knew that I wouldn't stay submissive, which of course would be all the fun.

"Any time, beautiful, any time," he said with hooded eyes.

Oh my. That gives me some delicious ideas. And he's into that for sure. What fun!

By the time we got to the alley where the occult store was located, it was midnight. But that was okay; the store didn't have hours of operation. It was open whenever you wanted it. However, the doorway was difficult to find at night. It was naturally hidden in the shadows.

"Hmmm, I am not sure which of these panels is the right one. I have a spell that will show us the right doorway."

"*Omina patchu fleeses,*" and a light glowed around the doorway, showing where it was on a blank wall under an overhang.

"I would never have seen that!" exclaimed Rick.

"No, it's hidden from human eyes," I said.

Pushing the door open, I grasped Rick's hand and walked in, pulling him inside with me. As soon as he cleared the door, it snapped shut and disappeared.

"Esperanza?" I asked the empty space. "I am back for more research, and I brought a supernatural friend with me. May we enter?"

All Rick could see was a hazy space in front of them that didn't let him focus on what was behind it. It was like looking through gauze.

The disembodied voice said, "Yes, you may enter. Mr. Rick Benal, since this is your first time here, please obey the rules and go only where I tell you. Otherwise, you may find yourself in the wrong place with no way to return."

"Was that a threat?" asked Rick, his fangs extending.

"No, just a statement of fact," said the disembodied voice.

"Come on, big guy, it's not Esperanza that is the threat, it's the store itself. You can get horribly lost here and end up in a different dimension," I explained. "Esperanza, please take us to the same location I was at a few days ago."

"Follow the light, please," said the voice.

I turned to Rick and told him to hang on to my hand. Under no circumstance was he to let go. I turned forward and we noticed a ball of light was now floating in front of me near the floor. I took one step and the gauze in front of us dissolved and suddenly we could see forward. It was fantastical. Books and shelves, and odd things were everywhere. It was a cornucopia of oddities and occult objects.

As we wove through the store following the ball of light, Rick's eyes were peeled, his head on a swivel trying to take it all in.

"I have no idea what most of these things are. They are amazing," he said.

Eventually we arrived at the armoire. I pulled the door open and behind was a whole room.

"Wow, that felt like we were leaving the store and entering some other place entirely," said Rick.

"In a way we were. Each 'room' is really another pocket dimension," I explained. The room in front of us stretched larger as we walked.

"How is it possible that the room is larger inside than outside?"

"Magic."

In the middle of the room was a table and a lamp. I put my bag down on the table and turned to him with a big smile on my face.

"Wow, your eyes are like huge saucers!" I cried. "No need to be frightened!"

"I'm not frightened, but I am excited and fascinated. Are we still in the store?"

"Nope, when we entered the armoire, we passed into a different dimension," I said nonchalantly. "It's how the store works. None of these particular books are for sale though, so we cannot remove them."

"Bummer," Rick said. "Okay, where do we start?"

I walked over to the shelves and fingered the books on the shelves.

"I'm looking for historical accounts of the Olde Ones. It's spelled with an 'e' as in O-L-D-E. If you can scan the shelves for me with your eyes that are so much better at seeing than mine, and grab anything that looks like a likely candidate, I'll start reading and making notes."

"Will do."

Finding more books was not going to be difficult, so I sat down with that first book I had and continued reading. There was a section on the problems they encountered with inter-species breeding that I thought was interesting.

"The primitive Clovis people did not seem to be very compatible with our species even though we appeared similar physically. They could relate to us, and we could produce offspring. However, children born to their females were often deformed and not viable. In the worst cases, they would get illnesses, and have diseases indicating that our DNA was somehow corrupting theirs.

In the best cases, the children were whole looking, but their minds were unhinged somehow and exhibited mental illnesses that our species hadn't seen in tens of thousands of millennia. This was indeed sad. The human DNA from these couplings became destabilized.

The humans didn't eliminate those children as we would have on our home world. They kept them alive, claiming they were special. We did not stay long enough to track what happened to these humans, but fear that they created their own line of descendants and passed along those corrupted genes.

The children born to our females did not suffer these fates. They were born whole and immortal. They had all the characteristics of their mother's species—the same vitality, speed, strength, better senses and reflexes. Over the time we were in contact with the Clovis People, we saw many of their generations die. They had very short life spans. Children born to our females from Clovis males did not couple with anyone in our community, they had sex with other humans. Those children were not born immortal. Again, the females had healthy children, but the males did not. There was something about the females that preserved the integrity of the DNA and prevented corruption.

We never found out what it was. However, we did discover accidentally that the children of our females could become immortal. A serum that was a retrovirus could rewrite their DNA and change specific chromosomes that turned them from mortal humans fully into us.

After these unsettling consequences, we decided to stay away from humanity. Our family group stopped growing, but we had enough to sustain ourselves. With roughly seventy-five new members of our family, this new generation would see us into the future.

There the account stopped. It was like the author either gave up documenting their lives, or died. So I had learned more, who they were, where they came from, and how their DNA got into the population. We were just going to have to find another book from this group perhaps.

"Hey, Lora," called Rick. "Lora! Earth to Lora!"

"Oh! Sorry! I was deep in thought," I said.

"I think I've found another book. It's entitled *Genealogy of Family Unit 32.* The front of the book lists North America as their base of operations."

"That sounds promising. Bring it here please."

Scanning through the book, I saw notations that matched the story I had just finished reading. This account listed people's names, who they had copulated with, and eventually procreated with. Since they listed both males and females, this information would make my search easier.

I followed the female lines down to their last entries in an effort to perhaps find a modern name. Each immortal female had hundreds of lovers, and dozens of children. On average, every seventy-five to a hundred years.

The last births listed happened better than twelve hundred years ago. That was still a long time for humans, and they might not show up in any human genealogy books. But it was something. Again, I followed the women, because mitochondrial DNA was inherited from the mother and passed to daughters, that was the DNA that carried the immortal genes that could be awakened.

"Look at this, Rick," I said, pointing out the location of one of the descendants.

"Oh, it is describing an archipelago of islands that sounds a lot like the Caribbean, the largest island which could be Cuba. That is where one of the immortal women lived and gave birth to an immortal child."

"She was immortal and had a child by an immortal?"

"Then the child was born immortal?" asked Rick.

"They developed a serum that they injected into the child to change his or her DNA into immortal," I explained. "This is the last child of this particular immortal woman. If we can follow the trail of children, we may find a near relative for you."

Chapter 24

— Mark

If only I could walk through walls.

I woke up dreaming that thought. I crashed awake if that's possible. Startled by my actions in the dream of beating against the wall. At the last moment, I crashed through the wall into wakefulness.

Of course, being awake didn't mean my brain was connected. Everything was fuzzy. The last thing I remember was leaving the cell and becoming solid by Falon. I remember holding her, she was injured. I was rocking her as my body started becoming transparent. *Think!* I told myself, *what happened?*

Concentrating with the little brain power at my disposal, I focused on being solid. I was strong, so strong! Oh! I remember picking someone up and throwing them. *Why did I do that?* What was it? I stood up and was pacing around my cell.

She was attacked!

At that thought, I struck the wall with both fists and they sank into the rock.

Blinking in shock, I pulled them out quickly and looked at the wall. My eyesight had adapted a little to the extreme darkness. I now sort of saw shapes. But I felt the wall where my fists were and found nothing different. I was sure I'd felt my fists go through the stone.

How can that be?

I tried to calm myself down, but my heart rate was off the scale.

Walking around the cell got my blood moving, which helped to clear the fuzziness in my head. Now, I remember: I had felt Falon's fear acutely. I needed to project to her, but I was as a solid object rather than a spectral object. *Did I kill him?* I remember throwing him against a tree, and wanting to rip him to shreds. *Oh god, please don't let that be the case. It will be a mess to cover up.*

If what I thought happened actually did, then what I can do with the projection can be changed by pushing more power into it. *Huh!* Calm projections let me be inside her head; add more energy and I can create a visible, but transparent projection; and still more energy lets me project a solid projection that can make physical contact.

Normally, when I project, I was very calm and focussed, not the raging bull I had been then. I have not had that level of power to push into a projection before.

Somehow I had managed to project when I was fully angered. *What was the difference? Falon!* She was the difference. I had felt her terror. It was such a strong emotion that when combined with mine it let me materialize next to her? *Maybe I can project myself out of this cell.*

I sat on the floor again, focussed, and started slowing down my heart. As calm permeated   being again, I was able to reach out with my mind and see myself sitting on the floor. Now, my astral self moved over to the wall. I thought about my power increasing as I held up my hands to the wall. I *saw* them push through the stone in my mind first and then pushed against the wall. My hands passed through!

Since I'd never tried this before, I didn't know what the results would be. I was up to my elbows through the stone right now. *Should I go farther?*

I took a step and my body came in contact with the stone and started to phase through it.

The feeling of my hands passing through the stone was unlike anything else. I could feel the material contacting every millimeter of my skin. Pushing through hurt too. So I knew when my hands were not in the stone anymore. I could move them freely.

As soon as my torso started going through the stone, I felt like a gorilla was sitting on my chest. I could barely breathe. But that was silly; my projection didn't need to breathe. I kept pushing, and eventually I was on the other side of the stone.

I found myself in a corridor. Dim lighting ran along the ceiling, showing me a very long distance. At the end though was an exit sign. Thank goodness for building codes. I started running down the hall. When I got to the end, there were stairs going up.

Déjà vu again. How did I know this?

I ran up the stairs and reached another door. Going through it, I found a building that had offices and another hallway lined with doors. This hallway was brightly lit and wide. The light was hard on my eyes after all the time in the darkness. Even my projection was having difficulty. Looking for another exit, I wandered down the hallway.

Finally, I spotted another exit. I ran the distance and pushed through the door. *Outside!* The sun was blinding. So it was daytime, and by the position of the sun, near midday. I took a deep breath and smelled mountain air, clean, crisp, and sweet.

Okay, so now I know how to get out of here. I just need to escape this room.

I brought my astral projection back. It reunited with my body and I opened my eyes.

Now, how do I get my body through the wall? My rage was out of control when my fists pounded into the stone. So that was the key to power. Raw emotion. All I had to do was tap into my feelings and reach out to Falon. Her fear drove me mad.

With my eyes glowing and my fangs fully extended again, I stoked my rage, but this time I was in control. I amped myself up, feeling the power building. It energized every cell in my body until my fingertips felt like they were sizzling.

Walking over to the stone wall, I focussed my power into my hands and pushed against the stone. I felt the same sense of pushing through very dense material, and it was pushing back on my skin. But my fists were making progress. I opened my eyes and saw that my arms were in the wall up to my elbows.

Quelling a split second of fear that I would become stuck, I amped up my anger and focused again. Making a considerable leap of faith, I pushed my whole body to the wall and felt myself slip into the stone.

As my chest entered, there was that gorilla sitting on my chest again. This time I held my breath and continued to push. My upper torso was through—just my hips and feet to go. As soon as they were clear, I slumped to the floor in exhaustion. That had taken nearly everything I had. Taking inventory of my body, I verified everything was there and working. Well, I didn't know if everything worked yet. But I had ten toes and ten fingers. So far, so good.

Now to follow the same route to get out of the building. Falon, I'm coming!

Just as my projection did, I found the exit at the end of the corridor and the stairs upstairs. However, when I got to the top of the stairs, there were all kinds of people in the office section I had seen. This was different from when I came through here as a projection. *Why? No time to figure this out just now, but I will later.*

How was I going to get past all those people?

Perhaps I could shadow walk. After all, I wasn't blind here. I knew where I was going, and I could "see" it in my mind's eye.

Again, harnessing the power of focused thought, I shadow walked to the outer door I had found.

I was in a small entranceway. The door was in front of me, but before going through it I listened carefully to see if there was anyone close by. Confirming that I was alone, I pulled open the door and exited.

Just as my projection discovered, it was daylight, but I think it was late afternoon. I smelled mountain air too. The sound of traffic told me that there were likely humans nearby and therefore some sort of town. *That will be how I get away.* I appeared to be on a roof at the moment. The surface under my feet was gravel. There was a wall to my left that had no windows. There was nothing overlooking the roof, so I was basically out of sight of anyone. I saw that there was a street with a fair amount of traffic to the right side of the building.

I decided to take a minute, catch my breath, and see if I could reach Falon now. I sat on the roof with my back against the wall and thought of Falon. I could feel her fear. It was a beacon to me.

I found her in bed sleeping. I entered her dreams.

She was walking down a straight, smooth path. There was a bench up ahead and she decided to sit on it. I touched her shoulder slightly and she turned around and looked up into my eyes. I lifted a transparent hand and caressed her cheek.

I wrapped her in love in the dream and made sure she would heal from her trauma. When I left her dreams, she was content and smiling in blissful sleep.

Now to get out of here. Keeping close to the building, I walked over to the edge of the roof. I was about three stories up. There was no ladder or staircase down to the ground. I either jumped or went back inside.

Seeing as going inside was not an option, I prepared to jump down. I should be able to land safely, as it was only about thirty feet.

Here goes nothing!

Taking a grip of the edge of the building, I vaulted over the ledge and dropped down to the ground. Landing on my feet, I rolled once over my back and ended up in a superhero pose.

So that's how they do that.

Standing up, I brushed myself off and started walking down the main street. On the corner, I found a coffee shop with a phone booth outside.

Wow, a phone booth. They're rare!

Watching for cars, I crossed the street and went inside the phone booth. There was a directory. Another piece of luck. Opening it up, I saw that the book was for the town of Sumpter, Oregon. *Huh! I'm in Eureka! (*a TV program in 2006 set in this town). That explained the mountain air.

Checking my clothes, I realized I didn't have any identification with me. Neither did I have my wallet or money. So how would I get home to Falon? I could walk into a police station and let them know that I'd just escaped from being kidnapped. But that would put the family in the crosshairs of the humans. *Can't do that.*

I couldn't call Gwen. She was part of it somehow. That was disappointing.

Rick? Could I call Rick? He was certainly in a position to loan me some money.

Okay, I'd call Rick. I remembered his number luckily, and started a collect call. Hopefully, Rick would accept the charges and the operator would put me through.

"Hello?"

"Mr. Benal, will you accept the charges from Mark Chisholm?" asked the operator.

"Certainly," said Rick. "Go ahead."

"Hi? Mark?" asked Rick.

"Yes, Rick, thanks for accepting the charges. I'm in a bit of a pickle," I said.

"No problem. What's up?"

"Well, I find myself in Sumpter, Oregon, without my wallet, ID, or money. Can you help me?" I asked.

"Oh man, sure. What do you need?"

"Well, enough to get back to Falon," I answered.

"How about I book you a flight from there to Kansas and send you some money? Is there a Western Union in that town?"

"Yes, there is, but no airport. I'll tell you what. If you can send a thousand dollars, I can manage myself."

"Okay."

"Thanks very much. Bye."

First things first, I needed to contact Falon. I needed a quiet place out of the way where no one would bother me while I was projecting. I walked down the main street until I found a park. There were some empty benches under some trees that would be perfect.

Stretching out on the bench, I pretended to take a nap. I closed my eyes and dropped into my meditation. Projecting myself now was easy. Finding Falon was second nature. It only took a moment before I felt her heart. I stopped and looked at where I was. Falon was awake and sitting up in bed. Her beautiful face was strained and tear streaked. It was clear that she was hurt and unhappy.

I felt my anger rising again, and my fangs started extending. The thought of her being hurt by anyone filled me with rage.

"*Falon*," I spoke into her mind.

"Mark?" She looked up and around. *"Is that you?"*

"Yes, love, it's me."

"Where are you?" she whispered.

"Apparently, I'm in a small town called Sumpter, Oregon," I answered.

"Did they release you?" she asked. *"Wait, you can contact me now, why not before?"*

"No, I escaped," I answered. *"Before, I was inside a building, in a cell underground. I wasn't able to get out with my projection when I tried. Not until I was able to materialize beside you. That is new though, and I'm not sure how I did that."*

"Then you're not safe yet, are you?" she asked.

"Not clear of trouble, no. But I'm okay right now. I'm more worried about you. Are you doing okay? Have you healed? Did you speak to the police?"

"I'm doing okay. I have healed, and yes I filed a report with the police. What happened? Oh my, I can't tell you like this. I will when I have you in my arms again, I promise. Know that I'm okay right now."

I wasn't really satisfied with that answer. I had to accept it though.

I knew the council had sent a thug after her, but I'm not going to tell her that yet. *"I don't like this. What did the police do to you?"*

"Just asked questions and took samples. Oh no, it wasn't your family. It was a customer," she quickly said.

I projected my senses so that I could touch her. A gentle caress on her cheek. I watched her smile and her head leaned into my caress.

"*It was you who came to me in my dream last night?*" she asked.

"*Yes, I felt your pain, and tried to comfort you.*"

"*It did. I felt loved and safe. Thank you,*" she said. "*What will you do next?*"

"*Rick is going to send me money, and I'll get back to you.*"

"*Mark, be careful!*" she cried.

"*I will,*" I assured her. Pulling back from her was difficult, but I had to get some plans into play. When I got back to myself and opened up my eyes, there were some kids standing around me, staring.

"Oh, his eyes just opened!" screamed one little girl.

"He's alive!" yelled a boy.

"Hey, mister, why do you have fangs?" asked another child.

Oh boy, my fangs must have come out while I was projecting to Falon, I thought to myself.

"I don't have fangs," I said. "See?" I opened my mouth to show them.

"You used to, I touched one of them when we thought you were dead," the child assured him.

"It's your imagination, little one. I don't have fangs, and I wasn't dead either. I was meditating. It's like a deep sleep," I explained, adding a tiny bit of compulsion to my voice to make sure the kid believed me.

Across the park, I heard a mother calling for children by name. The little group in front of me turned around and ran off, all except one.

"Mister, you shouldn't sleep on park benches. Only homeless people do that, and you wouldn't want to be homeless," the boy told me earnestly.

"You're absolutely correct. I wouldn't want that," I said. "Thank you for letting me know." I smiled.

Walking back to the payphone, I found a Western Union office nearby. It was only a few blocks away from the main drag. Figures, that sort of store would be in a less prosperous part of town.

When I walked into the store, there was no one at the desk. Ringing the bell, I waited until a bent-over elderly man came wobbling to the front.

"Can I help you, young man?" asked the clerk.

"Yes please," I said. "A friend of mine wants to send me some money. How do we go about doing that?"

The old gentleman looked at me askance but pulled a book out and asked me what the phone number was. I told him the friend's name was Rick Benal. When Rick answered, the clerk introduced himself, and asked Rick if he wanted to send this chap any money—looking at me for my name—then telling him.

"Yes, I need to send him some money, yes please," I heard Rick say on the other end.

The Western Union clerk proceeded to explain to him what to do. When I got off the phone, I turned to him and he let me know it would take about an hour for the money to clear, and to come back then.

Chapter 25

— Falon

A few months after my attack, I'd felt vindicated by the fact that the police arrested the German and he was sitting in prison. The case was very clear, especially because Interpol had a file on him too.

With a sigh of relief, I could get on with my life. Mark wasn't home yet, but I was expecting him soon.

Right now, I was facing Kansas summer weather. You remember how the *Wizard of Oz* started? With a tornado. Tornado season had started in Kansas. From May to September you could spot one of those twisters destroying something. It was like the movie, except way scarier. The movie was quite realistic even though it didn't have the same CGI we do in the 21st century.

Hot, really hot weather, coupled with very steamy thunderstorms, brought about the perfect combination of things to create one of these monsters. From my hotel room, I could see quite a distance over the other buildings. As I said, it was a big horizon.

On the news today, we were told to be on the lookout for tornadoes to hit my suburb of Kansas City. *Wait, I thought tornadoes didn't hit cities.* Nope, that was an urban legend. They hit cities; it was just rare. There was so much open land out here in the middle of the United States, and the settlements were so far apart, that tornadoes usually didn't hit anything urban.

But when they did, they destroyed everything in their path.

Staring out the window, my mind went back to Mark. His call last week was proof he was alive and well. He was still in trouble, though. *What happens when the family discovers he's escaped?* Rick sent him a thousand dollars in cash by Western Union. Hopefully, that would help him get home to me. In this day and age, it was difficult to do anything without an ID or a credit card. *Does he have contacts that can get him new ones?* He couldn't go to the family for help, that was for sure.

Not really feeling like being with people, I decided to work from my hotel room. Maybe go to the pool later. I cleared it with the programming lead and the client. They knew how to reach me if they absolutely had to.

I ordered room service for brunch and got out my laptop and my files and spread them out on the table. It was placed by the window, so I could watch outside while I worked.

The knock on my door signaled my food had arrived. Getting up and opening the door, the bellhop pushed in the trolley. I passed him a ten-dollar bill and closed the door after him.

I wheeled the food to the table. I had ordered blueberry pancakes, scrambled eggs, OJ, coffee, and bacon. It smelled wonderful. The pancakes were done to perfection—light and fluffy. They soaked up the maple syrup nicely too.

There was another knock on my door. "Did you forget something?" I asked as I walked toward the door. Opening the door, the person on the other side pushed the door in, completely knocking me over.

I screamed, but that did no good as a hand clamped over my mouth. I remembered what happened not too long ago. My stomach curdled and the dread nearly made me pass out. This time I wasn't drugged though, so I fought like a she-devil.

Putting my Krav Maga to good use, I had one on the floor while I was trying to do the same to the other. I almost had him in a hold when I felt a prick in my neck and everything went black.

I came back as an assailant was holding me from behind and I couldn't see who it was. It was a male though and immortal, because he was as strong as me. I felt my hands being bound, and my feet too. The next thing was a bag being pulled over my head. I could no longer see.

A second rough pair of hands put a piece of tape over my mouth, and then the two of them picked me up and carried me. I struggled as much as I could but with my hands and feet bound there wasn't much I could do. I was afraid we were going into the bedroom. I didn't want to go through that again.

I heard the hotel room door close behind me and we were still moving. So they were taking me out of the hotel? I felt the rhythmic footsteps of the men as they walked down stairs. So they were going down the stairways to be secretive. Another door opened, and I smelled cars and tires, so we must be in the underground parking garage. The next thing I knew, I was being shoved into something that had a hard interior and I heard the lid of a trunk slam closed. I was in the trunk of a car. I was being kidnapped!

I knew, as surely as I know myself, that it was the family taking me. Just like they took Mark. Why, I had no bloody good reason. Except perhaps to get him to heel. If they were going to use me as bait, that would work. So they knew he had escaped and they were trying to lure him to them now.

Oh my, Mark, be careful.

The car hadn't started moving yet. What were the kidnappers waiting for? Another door opened, then the trunk opened again. I felt another sting, this time in my leg. *They injected me with something*, I thought. And then black. Everything went black.

I woke up and the first thing I realized was that I was sitting in a hard chair and my hands were tied to the chair. The bag was still over my head. The room smelled damp and moldy. So it was a basement of some kind.

Perhaps it was the hotel's basement?

Nah, that makes no sense. They put me in a car. Think, Falon, think.

A door opened behind me and I heard footsteps approaching. My stomach clenched with nerves. The bag was pulled off my head, and that made me sneeze. Another person turned on a bright light and shone it directly into my eyes.

That hurt! Squinting, I try to see beyond the light but couldn't. So I closed my eyes again to avoid the pain of the light.

"You're awake," came the voice. I think it was a woman, but it was difficult to tell.

"You're going to tell us where Mark Chisholm is," said the voice.

"I don't know where he is," I replied honestly.

"He left our facility five days ago. Has he contacted you?"

"He called me last week," I answered.

"Where was he?"

"He didn't say," I lied.

"That's a lie," the voice said. "I can smell lies, so there is no point in trying to lie to me."

"He told me he was in Eureka," I said.

"Eureka?" was the query.

"Yup. Eureka, Oregon," I said. Let them chew on that. *I was referencing a television program from 2006. The fictional town was based on an actual place, just a different name.*

"Did he tell you what he had planned?"

"No."

"Are you sure?"

"Yes."

"Did he ask for anything?"

"Yes, he asked me to send him some money."

"Did you?"

"Yes."

"How?"

Darn, then they'll be able to trace it. "Through Western Union."

"Good, excellent. Remi, trace that money transfer now."

"Yes, Councilwoman."

Huh, so she was a member of the council. Was this the family council? Did they have a gov?

"Falon, tell me how you met Mark and when."

I don't want to tell them anything, but I felt this strange sensation slide over my head like a stocking being pulled down. My head felt squeezed and my vision went slightly blurry. *Were they using compulsion on me?* I shook my head to try to clear the sensation. It wouldn't go away.

"Falon you must answer because I've compelled you to."

I tried sealing my lips closed. If I didn't speak, I wouldn't give away anything.

"Falon you must speak, now." I felt the stocking around my head tighten until it felt like I couldn't breathe.

Mark and I had agreed on a storyline that was the truth for public consumption, but didn't include everything to be "the" story in case the family ever challenged us. So that is what I told her now. It included our first year together in 2016, reuniting in New York, and then meeting again in Atlanta. It included making love and being bitten once, but I didn't go into that detail.

"Did you have sex with Mark in New York?"

"No, we just talked. I didn't know who he was yet."

"When was your first sexual encounter?"

"It was in Montreal."

"Did Mark bite you during that sexual encounter?"

"No," I answered.

"When did he bite you?"

"The first week I was in Atlanta, Georgia."

"Did you have unprotected sex?"

"Yes, amazing sex. We both lost control completely, and he bit me then. I didn't know what it was, though.."

"When did he tell you who he was?"

"Well, when I woke up, because the bite had knocked me out for a few hours, he told me he had to explain some things. That's when he came clean about what he was, what the bite meant, and what it would do."

"What happened next?"

"We sort of broke up because I was furious."

"When did that change?"

"Just before my birthday."

"Did you consent to be bitten by him?"

"I did. I asked him to. That's when we made love, and it was a different experience. It drew something out of him, and I gained something. It's like we truly became one body."

"Have you experienced anything happening to your body? Anything different?"

"Not really."

"Humph," came the response. The councilwoman then walked out of the room I was in and the door was closed. At least they didn't leave me in total darkness. I could barely see my hands.

But I did hear what sounded like a freight train coming a little while later. It was a roar of some kind. And then I started to feel vibrations through the floor. The building was shaking. The roar intensified. Then I heard the wind and the crash of things being flung around. Somewhere, objects were being thrown into glass, and against buildings. I could hear the smashing and clangs of impacts above the roar.

The shaking was starting to rattle the chair I was in, to the point that it was moving along the floor. As the noise intensified, the ceiling started to move up and down like it was breathing. It was only ceiling tiles, but that meant the floor above it was also moving. Geez! There wasn't anything I could take shelter under down here.

The door to the room opened and someone shouted to get out.

"I can't! I'm tied up!" I shouted back.

The person ducked inside and untied one hand and ran away.

"Thanks a lot," I said sarcastically. But it gave me one hand to untie the other.

The roar was so loud it seemed like the train was going to be on top of me any second. The ceiling was jumping and buckling. Suddenly, a piece of the ceiling ripped away, letting in a little light.

"Oh God, that's not good," I said as I saw the sky through that opening in the ceiling. "Come on, Falon, let's get out of this chair!" I encouraged myself. Frantically, I was trying to get the last knot undone with one hand. It wasn't as easy as you would think. At least I could stand up and move. That's what I did. I lifted the chair over my head thinking that might protect me from being hit by flying debris.

The roaring was thunderous now. With the chair over my head, I stood in the doorway. That's where you're supposed to stand in a tornado, right? Strongest part of the building and all that?

The floor ripped away. I could see it being swept up by the wind and carried into the funnel cloud. Now flying debris was being whipped around in circles and it was coming down through the ceiling. More of the ceiling disappeared until it was just floor joists. The debris started raining down on me, along with baseball-sized pieces of hail.

A 2x4 slammed like a spear through the wall to my right, narrowly missing me by three inches. It went all the way into the hallway and the wall across from me. A car landed on the ceiling and crashed through the floor joists. The adjacent wall buckled under the weight.

Throwing the chair away, I realized that I was going to get trapped down here if I didn't move now. The way toward the right was blocked now. I saw walls being crushed with debris.

I started making my way toward the left. The wall behind me collapsed under the weight above it, and I barely escaped being crushed. Slowly, I made my way down the hallway; another wall collapsed in front of me. Then a couch landed on top of the wall right above me. *That could make a shelter to hide under,* I thought.

I pulled the couch off the debris and turned it upside down. It created a small hollow where I could hide, hopefully in safety. I crouched down under the couch and listened to the sound of debris being tossed around and walls being dropped all around me. Luckily, the sofa saved me from being crushed, but I was trapped. I tried to lift the sofa up when something very heavy landed on it crushing me to the ground. I heard my leg snap as I crumpled under the weight. I curled up as best I could in the smaller space.

I'm going to die here, I realized. Tears started flowing down my face unbidden. "I'm still in Kansas, it seems."

Excerpt from Book 4

IMMORTAL VICTORY

1- Rescued!

I came back to consciousness like coming out of a very deep sleep. You know that point at which the dream you've been having ceases to feel like a dream and you know that you've been asleep? It feels like it should be dark but light is coming through your eyelids.

The last place I remembered flashed through my mind: hiding under an upside-down sofa, being buried alive by a building.

My eyes were closed. I didn't want to open them, so I kept them closed and took an inventory of my body, what I felt and heard.

I felt no pain. That was good, because my legs hurt like crazy before. Or maybe not good. *Am I alive?*

I didn't feel twisted in a strange position. That was also good.

I could hear voices! Lora and Mark talking quietly nearby. *I'm not buried anymore!*

Tears welled up in my eyes in gratitude for not being dead. Reflecting a moment on what happened, I realized my last week had been harrowing.

First, I got kidnapped and interrogated, then buried by a tornado. *Wait, where am I?*

I cracked my eyes open and saw I was in a hospital bed, machines and tubes all around me. *Hmmm.* This might not be a good thing either. *If I heal too quickly, that will expose my secret.*

I tried to speak but my throat was so dry that it came out as a rasp, barely loud enough for me to hear myself. I realized there was a device in my hand with a button on it. Probably a call button, but one that would call a nurse. I didn't want to do that.

While I was trying to figure out what to do, Lora popped her head around the doorjamb and looked in. When she saw my eyes were open, her face broke into a big grin. She walked toward me, pulling Mark by the sleeve behind her.

"Oh my Goddess, we were so worried!" she started. "But you're awake now, so we can get you out of here."

I tried to speak again, and Lora got the message. A straw was placed between my lips and I gratefully sucked on it until cool liquid poured into my mouth. I swirled it around some before swallowing to lubricate my tongue.

"I'm so glad to see you!" I blurted out. Tears, again welling in my eyes, spilled over and ran down my face into my ears. Lora wiped them away.

"You're all right now. We've got you."

"Mark, you escaped!" I whispered.

"Yes, and when I got back here you were missing," he said. "I called Lora, and she got on the next flight down here to help me."

"I still can't believe I survived the tornado," I said. "I absolutely thought I was going to die there, buried under ceiling tiles and concrete." I shuddered with the memory.

"The firefighters who rescued you were the heroes," said Lora. "They found you buried under an entire building. Somehow a sofa was enough to keep you alive and give you enough air that you survived until they found you."

"I know I'm immortal," I whispered. "But that's still new. I don't instinctively think that way. When concrete buildings fell down on my head and I couldn't fight my way out, it was terrifying. I really thought I was going to die.

"I remember being in so much pain," I added. "I'm so grateful to the firefighters who risked their own lives to find me and rescue me."

"You're fine now," said Lora. "In fact, you're all healed, which is the problem. Mark and I were talking about it."

"How long have I been here?" I asked.

"Two days," said Lora. "You were brought in two days ago with crush injuries. They had to reset your legs and do some surgery to repair some internal damage."

"Was that necessary?" I asked.

"No, it wasn't," answered Mark. "At least not the surgery. Resetting your legs was, or they wouldn't have healed right."

"I need to leave here, don't I?"

"Yup, sooner than later," said Mark. "The doctors make their rounds at 10:00 a.m. If they discover that the surgical site is gone and that the bones have healed, they'll be doing more tests … and we don't want that."

"What time is it?"

"It's coming on 7:30 a.m.," Lora answered. "So we have a little time to get you out of here."

"So what's the plan?" I asked.

"I'm going to insist that you be allowed to leave with me," said Mark. "I will tell them I have private nurses who can do the job better. I will get the papers for you to sign so that you can do so."

"Don't insult them, please," I said. "After all, they were the first responders who helped me."

"No, I'll be the arrogant rich prick and take the blame, don't worry."

"I've brought some clothes for you," said Lora. "You'll have to leave in a wheelchair because both your legs are in casts."

I looked down at my body and gasped at the fact that both my legs were encased in plaster.

"Geez, how did I not notice that?" I asked.

"Well, the fact that you're lying flat and not in pain would let your mind skip over that," said Mark.

"So, like I said, we take you out in a wheelchair," said Lora.

"What about my boss?"

"I've called him, and you'll be staying at the hotel and taking a few days off at least," said Mark. "I may even arrange for you to return home to Montreal to convalesce. We'll see."

"Mark, you go get those release papers and I'll get her dressed," said Lora.

"Come on, hun, I've got a dress for you to put on so we don't have to argue with the casts."

As we struggled to get me upright, at least enough to slip the dress over my head, Mark went and spoke to the woman at the nurses' station. I heard a heated argument, then calm voices. Mark returned a few minutes later.

"I had to use compulsion on her to give me the papers," said Mark. "They were not going to let me take you out of the hospital." He handed them to me. I signed them and gave them back.

"Is that going to be a problem?" I asked.

"I hope not," he said, walking away as he took the papers back to the nurses' station. By that time, Lora was back with a wheelchair. After Lora helped me out of my hospital gown and into the dress, Mark lifted me off the bed and set me down in the chair. That was easy. Lora scooped up all my tattered belongings that had been cut off me, plus the jewelry that had been removed when they brought me into Emergency, and put them all in a shopping bag.

"After you, sir," she said to Mark, with a smile.

Mark wheeled me out of the room, and the three of us moved down the corridor toward the elevator. The door opened, we got on and made it down to the hospital's main lobby. Crossing the lobby toward the main door as calmly and as quickly as we could, we were nearly clear of the sliding doors when I heard a voice yelling after us.

"Stop! You can't leave the hospital yet! You've not been cleared!" said someone.

We didn't stop or turn around but just kept going out to the parking lot. Mark lifted me into the front passenger seat that was waiting for us, while Lora dumped my shopping bag into the trunk and got into the back seat with Mark. There was a stranger, a handsome stranger, driving the car.

"Hello, I'm Falon," I introduced myself.

"Hello, Falon, I'm Robert Andrews and I'll be your driver today."

When we got back to the hotel, Mark kept up the appearance of me having two broken legs. He carried me into the hotel and up to the room. On the way through the lobby, several people stopped momentarily to give us condolences and well wishes to get better. I thanked them as Mark breezed by quickly without stopping.

When Lora opened the door to my room, I discovered it was a mess.

"Oh my God! What happened to our room?" I yelled.

"It appears that after they grabbed you, someone came back here and tore this place apart looking for something," said Mark. "We don't know what it was."

"Yeah, the kidnappers were smart enough to put a Do Not Disturb sign on the door handle, so the hotel staff wouldn't go in and discover the mess," said Lora. "That's the only reason I found the room like this."

"The first thing we did was to tell the hotel not to clean the room, and to leave it just as it is so that my security could conduct an investigation because you had been abducted from the room."

"That makes sense," I said. "But look at the mess they've left! Everything is upside down and ripped apart!"

"It's only stuff, Falon," Mark said. "You are the important one to me, and you're okay."

"I agree, it's just stuff," said Lora. "We'll get it cleared up right away."

"Actually, Lora, wait a bit. I need your help to release her from these casts."

"What does that entail?" I asked.

"Without a saw, I'll have to break them," said Mark. "Lora is going to hold you while I break the plaster."

"Oh, just that, eh?"

I lay face-down on the sofa and Lora held me while Mark applied pressure to the cast from the back of my leg. He forced it to bend at the knee until it cracked and he could peel it off in pieces. Boy, did it make a mess! There was plaster dust everywhere.

"I guess that's why they use a saw to remove them in the hospital," I noted.

He grinned at me. "I don't have a saw small enough."

Once the casts were off, they encouraged me to stand up.

"You're sure I can?" I asked. "I mean, I had compound fractures in both legs. Have they really healed?"

"Yes, mostly healed. I saw the x-rays they took this morning. You should be able to put weight on them now. It's why we had to get you out of there."

"Oh!"

Holding on to Lora and Mark, they eased me up until I was standing. There was little pain, and my legs were sort of working. *Wow!* I looked for the stitches I had in my stomach; they were gone too. So that would have been a problem.

"Well, thanks guys for getting me out of there. Now, where do we start here?"

"You look for all the valuables: laptops, phones, technology, money, et cetera. See if any of it was taken," said Mark. "Lora, you go through all her clothes to see if anything was destroyed. I'll look at all the furniture and assess the damage."

Pillows had been torn apart. Desk drawers had been pulled out and dumped on the floor. I went looking for my purse and briefcase. I last left them in the bedroom on the empty side of the bed because I had been working there. Going into the bedroom, it was clear immediately that my briefcase was gone and everything inside it as well.

"Well my laptop, phone, and other tech, as well as my files, have been taken," I reported. "Why would they take my files? I need to let my boss know."

I went to the hotel phone and dialed my boss's number in Montreal.

"Peter Prudhomme's office, how may I help you?"

"Ah, is Peter there? It's Falon."

"Oh, Falon, are you okay? We heard about the tornado and that you ended up in the hospital."

"Yeah, I'm fine, a few scratches. I was lucky. I was saved by a sofa and some firefighters."

"Good to hear. Peter is down in Kansas right now. Shall I get him to call you?"

"No, I can call his phone. Thanks."

"Bye, take care of yourself!"

"Thanks!"

Off the phone, I heard Lora telling Mark that all of the clothes she had found had been ripped apart like they were looking for something.

I called Peter's cell phone.

"Peter speaking."

"Peter, it's Falon."

"Falon, how are you doing?"

"I'm fine. I just need a few days off, I think. But that's not why I'm calling. I need to tell you that my laptop and all my tech was taken from my hotel room. In fact, while I was trapped in the tornado, someone ransacked my room. It doesn't make sense. I have filled out a police report. I'm not sure why, but they also took the files I had with me that I was working on. They also have the float of money that I had."

"So how much cash is gone?"

"About five hundred dollars."

"That's not too bad. Easily replaced. So is your tech. I'll have another laptop sent down for you today—they'll send it to the office. Anything else gone?"

"Apparently all my clothes are ripped to shreds. It seems they were looking for something, but I can't imagine what."

"Use the company card to go and replace your business wardrobe."

"Are you sure?"

"Yes, it's the least we can do."

"Thanks, Peter. That's awfully generous."

"And, Falon...?"

"Yeah?"

"Take a few weeks off. That's an order."

"Okay, boss."

I returned to the main room. It looked like a war had swept through. I stood there frozen, staring at the mess they made of our things, and I started crying my eyes out.

Mark wrapped his arms around me, comforting me.

"You should go to bed. You've been through an ordeal and you need to get your strength back. Let us take care of you."

"How are we going to explain no casts?"

"Lora has a good idea," said Mark.

"Tell them that you have stainless steel pins in your legs. It's a new procedure that allows for very fast healing."

"Oh, that is a good idea. You know what, guys, my legs are tired and starting to hurt. I think I will go back to bed now."

Mark put me to bed and I fell asleep almost immediately. My last thought was: *At least my boss won't be expecting me back to work for a while*. My legs were still unsteady—but the fractures to my bones were healing quickly. Mark figured one more day and it'd be like they'd never happened. The two of them cleaned up as much as they could, took stock of what was taken, and what needed to be replaced.

What's Next?

Book 4 — Immortal Victory

- An old enemy surfaces to threaten the Immortals just as life seems to be settling down.

- Lora and Rick's romance deepens while they delve into the ancient past to discover more about the Immortals and where they come from.

- Falon launches a charity

- Travel to Switzerland

- Huge gala

About The Author

Linda Ashton Trott

Ms Trott, a native of Montreal, Canada, currently lives in the nation's capital with her husband of twenty-four years, their four cats, and eight Japanese Koi.

When not writing, Ms Trott can be found in their backyard relaxing by the pond or editing her husband's stories.

Ms Trott has always had an interest in all things supernatural, the occult, UFOs, aliens, and the paranormal. It seemed natural to combine one or more of these elements into a unique universe in which to tell interesting stories.

These are not children's stories. "It's funny, I never sat down with the intention of writing Adult books," Linda once said. "But here they are. I wanted to express physical love honestly without cutesy acronyms and vague names."

These stories contain explicit language and hot, steamy sex scenes that will leave you panting.

Books In This Series

The Immortal Stories Series

The Immortals are a race of beings that came to Earth many tens of thousands of years ago. Their stories stretch across time and have become woven into the history of humans. Their society is hidden from humans even though they live among them. Forbidden from developing romantic liaisons with humans, some break the rules and form close bonds and get married. But this always comes with consequences.

1 - Immortal Desire

One immortal and one human.

As Zisis's world collides with Falon's, she is left to cope and deal with the blowback. Their love affair is erotic, passionate, and stirs the soul, but it is ill-fated. This is a story of romance, heartbreak, hardship, and survival. The sex is hot and steamy, the highs euphoric, and the lows devastating.

2 - Immortal Fulfillment

What a twist! What has Mark done?

After a nasty life twist has her rethinking a relationship with her Texan, Falon needs to decide which direction to go. Is she back to square one? Certainly not! Between hurricanes, hot tub invites, and road trips with hot, sexy guys, there is plenty of action and adventure.

3 - Immortal Peril

The Family is NOT happy!

Lora meets Rick, a talented dessert chef in an up-and-coming restaurant in Atlanta, Georgia, while visiting her best friend, Falon, who is on contract work there. Lora and Rick hit it off in ways she can't believe—one hot weekend in Miami and she can't get him out of her mind. So, when invited to Atlanta again, this time by Rick, she doesn't hesitate!

When Mark disappears without a trace, Falon is left to find out what happened.

4 - Immortal Victory

Out of the fire and into the frying pan!

Falon gets out of one problem only to find herself in danger again. An ancient enemy is targeting the immortals and will stop at nothing to eliminate them. Dodging assassins and traps, Falon decides to end homelessness, one person at a time.

Her BFF Lora discovers that true love sex generates magical energy while she looks for her ancestors.

Gwen finds a partner in Andrews.

5 - Immortal Hunt

Having just survived a coordinated attack from an ancient enemy, the immortals rejoice and celebrate their success. Attention turns toward locating their ancestors when a news item catches Lora's attention and gives her a very important clue to finding them. The immortals are off on a great adventure to distant places. Pirates, witches, time travel, spooky castles, and volcanic caves are some of the encounters happening this time. Don't miss out on the adventure!

6 - Immortal Nexus

New is old, and old is new

Surely, saving a coven of witches from a pocket dimension would be a highlight in life. But it's not. The immortals return home to everyday life; family, moving, school, raising teens, and of course, spicy lovemaking.

We meet a new character with a deep past. And when a new couple moves in across the street, Falon notices some familiar characteristics. She makes it her mission to meet the new neighbors.

Family matters are front and center in this story. The close-knit group of immortals is becoming a family, and some stories need sharing like Andrews' tale of being hired by aliens.

Justin and Rick finally open the new restaurant. It was a New Year's Eve celebration with a bang!

7 - Immortal Generation — Coming 2023

Short Stories

First Contact: An Immortal Origin Story

The Immortal's Origin Story started 33,000 years ago, when they arrived on Earth. *First Contact* follows the story of how the immortals meet the first humans and what happens when they interact and live together.

Praise for the Series

What are readers saying about this new series?

"Yet again I've got an ARC for this author and I've got to say that these books just get better and better. I loved this one [Book 6] and it is my favourite so far out of the series. There is now so many new people with there own stories that I don't think it will get boring any time soon. My favourite couple were Falon and Mark but I have quickly fallen in love with Margaret and Abeo and I didn't see the twist and turns right at the end. Brilliant book by a brilliant author."

... Sam ***** Amazon

"Linda Ashton Trott has a real gift for crafting intricate sex scenes that are highly charged and also entirely believable. She really brings you into the bedroom in a joyful way. The will-they-or-won't-they story keeps you wondering, right up to the plot twist at the end, which sets readers up for Book 2."

... Amy **** Amazon

"Ohhhhh! This book was good! Hot hot scenes with enough of a story in between to keep you hooked. We all need to

become Leopard Ladies! Nice quick read. Can't wait to read book 2 of the series!"

... *Josée **** Goodreads*

"Brilliant book loved the storyline and I couldn't put it down once I started. I loved the characters and got really absorbed in to their lives and feelings.

all I can say is Wow I loved every part of it (#3). I'm really sad that the book ended the way it did as I wanted to carry on reading and finding out what was going to happen. I love this series and all the characters. Hopefully there should be another one."

... *Sam ***** Amazon*

"Picking up where the first book ended, this installment of the series was the heroine's journey of self-discovery in order to make the right decisions for her, something I really enjoyed!

This book was sexy, fun and the character development was great! Ioved how the heroine slowly took back control of her life and found empowerment in her spontaneity."

...*Nikita **** Goodreads*

"wow! amazing, fast paced and enthralling new world! Wonderful characters that charmed me from the beginning. Honestly this was a wonderfully perfect read to help me escape from the world for a bit.

Amazing (#3). I love this world and it's characters. Great storyline and well written. This series has been amazing to read. Definitely need to pick them up."

... *Naomi ***** Amazon*

"Yet again I'm absolutely totally blown away by this book (#4). I love the characters and the story line. Linda has written a fantastic book with steamy scenes that I didn't think were possible but brilliant. I loved the fact that we're now starting to see smaller named characters have a bigger role. It's very well written and can't wait to read more of the series."

*...Sam ***** Amazon*

Being an Indie Author

I've chosen to publish independently. This means I don't have the big machine of a traditional publishing company behind me. Reviews are very important on Amazon because they determine how visible you are in the marketplace. That makes your review, and every other review I receive, the most important tool in my marketing toolbox. If you've enjoyed reading this book, please consider spending a few minutes leaving me a review on Amazon. It doesn't have to be long.

Thank you!

See my website at www.lindaashtontrott.com to join the mailing list. You will not be inundated with mail, I promise! It will let you know when the latest book is released and if there are freebies.

Visit my Amazon author's page at
https://www.amazon.com/~/e/B09TG29J19